Praise !
Carlton Me

"Easily the craziest, weirdest, strangest, funniest, most obscene writer in America."
—*GOTHIC MAGAZINE*

"Carlton Mellick III has the craziest book titles... and the kinkiest fans!"
—CHRISTOPHER MOORE, author of *The Stupidest Angel*

"If you haven't read Mellick you're not nearly perverse enough for the twenty first century."
—JACK KETCHUM, author of *The Girl Next Door*

"Carlton Mellick III is one of bizarro fiction's most talented practitioners, a virtuoso of the surreal, science fictional tale."
—CORY DOCTOROW, author of *Little Brother*

"Bizarre, twisted, and emotionally raw—Carlton Mellick's fiction is the literary equivalent of putting your brain in a blender."
—BRIAN KEENE, author of *The Rising*

"Carlton Mellick III exemplifies the intelligence and wit that lurks between its lurid covers. In a genre where crude titles are an art in themselves, Mellick is a true artist."
—*THE GUARDIAN*

"Just as Pop had Andy Warhol and Dada Tristan Tzara, the bizarro movement has its very own P. T. Barnum-type practitioner. He's the mutton-chopped author of such books as *Electric Jesus Corpse* and *The Menstruating Mall*, the illustrator, editor, and instructor of all things bizarro, and his name is Carlton Mellick III."
—*DETAILS MAGAZINE*

Also by Carlton Mellick III

Satan Burger
Electric Jesus Corpse
Sunset With a Beard (stories)
Razor Wire Pubic Hair
Teeth and Tongue Landscape
The Steel Breakfast Era
The Baby Jesus Butt Plug
Fishy-fleshed
The Menstruating Mall
Ocean of Lard (with Kevin L. Donihe)
Punk Land
Sex and Death in Television Town
Sea of the Patchwork Cats
The Haunted Vagina
Cancer-cute (Avant Punk Army Exclusive)
War Slut
Sausagey Santa
Ugly Heaven
Adolf in Wonderland
Ultra Fuckers
Cybernetrix
The Egg Man
Apeshit
The Faggiest Vampire
The Cannibals of Candyland
Warrior Wolf Women of the Wasteland
The Kobold Wizard's Dildo of Enlightenment +2
Zombies and Shit
Crab Town
The Morbidly Obese Ninja
Barbarian Beast Bitches of the Badlands
Fantastic Orgy (stories)
I Knocked Up Satan's Daughter
Armadillo Fists
The Handsome Squirm

SUNSET WITH A BEARD

CARLTON MELLICK III

ERASERHEAD PRESS
PORTLAND, OREGON

ERASERHEAD PRESS
205 NE BRYANT
PORTLAND, OR 97211

WWW.ERASERHEADPRESS.COM

ISBN: 1-933929-98-7

Author's Note

On 12/31/2000, New Year's Eve, I was drunk on Arrogant Bastard Ale, listening to Cauliflower Ass and Bob, sitting at my computer and waiting for my roommate to finish taking a dump so we could go out to a party. Then it happened . . . Via email, I received my first acceptance letter. It was for a collection of short stories called "Sunset with a Beard."

At first, I thought it was a mistake. I thought I was just too drunk to read the message properly . . . Well, I *was* too drunk to read *anything* properly, but the message was for real. I was going to get published. For the first time, somebody actually wanted to publish me. Yeah, *me!* The same drunk zombie movie bootlegger who dropped out of college one class away from graduation because he didn't want to take German anymore (even though he's half German citizen). This idiot was actually going to be a published writer. I couldn't believe it. Then, if I wasn't blissed out enough, I got another acceptance *two hours later!* It was for another collection called, "The Infant Vending Machine." Two acceptances in one day! I was having a pretty awesome New Year's Eve. I was on cloud-nine. My writing career was finally going somewhere.

Of course, it took several years for the book to actually come out and by the time it did I already had two other books in print, but still . . . I see it as my first book anyway, because it was the first to be accepted. Nothing beats the feeling of getting your first acceptance as a writer. Especially when you're already drunk.

These stories were all written between 1999-2000, when I was mostly focused on getting my name out there in science fiction magazines. Back then, I was trying to desguise my surreal/bizarro fiction as science-fiction, which didn't work out too well because most science-fiction editors said that science-fiction and surrealism just don't mix. Still, I tried passing my surreal stories off as science-fiction, with mediocre success.

When "Sunset with a Beard" was originally published, there

were 7 stories that were too surreal to be science-fiction and 7 stories that were too science-fictiony to be surrealism. I told readers that they had to figure out which ones were which. In the introduction, I gave readers this really lame challenge to see which story belonged to which genre. Winner got a free sandwich, or a free peg leg, or a free bulldog sled ride, or some stupid crap like that. I'm not giving away sandwiches this time. You can make your own damn sandwich. I'm just going to mention which stories are which in the table of contents.

As an added bonus, there are five new stories in this edition of the collection. Four of the stories, "The Third Planet from my Shoulder," "A Historyless People," "Filming the End of the World" and "Riverboat" were supposed to be published in the original release, but were cut. Three of them were instead published in "The Infant Vending Machine," but "Filming the End of the World" was trunked until now. The fifth bonus story, "God on Television," is another uncollected story that I've had lying around. It was the first story I wrote after this collection was published. Although uncollected, it has appeared in several anthologies over the years.

If you are wondering what is up with the cute little creature next to the girl on the cover of this book it is based on the artwork of Kristin Tercek, who does Cuddly Rigor Mortis. She does paintings and stuffed dolls of many cute creatures like the one on the cover. My favorite is the Lychee Zombie. Check out her stuff at **cuddlyrigormortis.com**.

So here you go, the re-release of "Sunset with a Beard." For those of you who missed it the first time around: I hope you like it. For those of you who already have the first edition and got this one for the bonus stories: what the hell is wrong with you? It's just five stories and they sure as hell aren't worth another $10. In fact, there was a reason why they were cut from the original edition in the first place, and it wasn't because they were too long.

- *Carlton Mellick III, 3/18/10*

CONTENTS:

THE
EARWIG FLESH FACTORY

It lives on a wrinkled hill made of rat-scabs and beetle shells, inky fluids draining from its exhaust pipes, creating puddles of a metal-scented tar substance.

It bubbles poisons into the dark-sizzling atmosphere, churshes out ear-twinging noises that reach all the way to the village of melted spiky shacks and yellow pepper-fruit trees.

It has a face on one side that mopes low to the ground, tilting. Its tongue dangles out of its wood-framed mouth, slithering, a lizard of a tongue.

An old woman walks up this red-rusty tongue leading to the factory, passing some chittering cockroach-bugs who hide under the silver-speckled dragonplants. Her face is covered with earwig flesh, as is her body and clothes—a purple material that is slime-shiny with a thick fatty odor. A group of village children stalk behind, splashing through the silvery puddles within their earwig flesh, tugging on the old woman's dress, begging for her to tell them a story.

"Please, please, Granmama," they cry.

"No, no," replies the old woman. "I must work with machines and produce the flesh."

"Just one story, Granmama," they cry.

"I must work with the machines and produce the flesh,"

replies the old woman.

She leaves the children on the front steps of the factory and marches across blue-veins on the cracked concrete to the machinery—greasy black boxes and ramps of teeth and rubber tubes. The old woman greets a pregnant woman at the machines without saying a word and then sends her home, replacing her position at the levers.

The children stare at the old woman through the broken windows, watching her make the machines go *whir-whir* and *churkle-choosh*. They pout in her direction, trying to cute her into telling another of her stories, but she is grumpy when working and not in the mood.

Please, please, please, their faces whine..

She ignores for several minutes, but then gives in. "Okay, come inside," she tells them through the earwig-ooze around her mouth. "I'll tell you a story while I work, but afterwards you have to go home."

The children agree and hop through the window, little drippy goblins circling around her and a rust-caked drill. She fiddles with the machines for a few minutes before even looking at them.

"Tell us about when the world changed, Granmama," they cry. "Tell us about the beautiful ugliness."

The old woman continues working with the machines as she speaks:

"It all started when the night sneezed on the world," her voice muffle-raspy and thin, "It was a hurricane explosion of black toxic snot that came from the sky and coated the face of the planet, stripped buildings into skeletons, sprayed a thick film of disease over the lakes and oceans, filled the sun with globs of pudding."

"Tell us about what happened to the people, Granmama."

"The people were dying one by one and liked it that way. Everyone said their goodbyes to each other and slowly died away. Nobody in the entire world tried to survive besides myself, they didn't think life was worth saving. They thought the world was too ugly to live in."

"But not you, Granmama," cry the children. "You thought the ugliness was beautiful."

"Yes," the old woman says, smiling underneath her slimy mask. "I thought it was *extremely* beautiful, more beautiful than before. The landscape was violent-colored, it was dark yet brilliant, silvery with metals and complex textures. I fell in love with it and wanted to live in it forever."

"Tell us how you did it, Granmama. Tell us how you survived."

"I figured out a way to transform human flesh into a coating that would protect my skin from the atmosphere and would absorb poison from my body, enabling me to breathe air and drink water without getting sick. I used the flesh of the people who were dying in the village, the ones on their death beds. I remember when I first put on the flesh. I looked so strange and . . . insecty."

"Like an earwig!" the children scream.

"Yes, like the peeling of an earwig."

"Tell us what happened when the flesh went rotten, Granmama."

"Well," says the old woman, "it didn't take much human flesh to create the earwig flesh, but after awhile I was running low on my supply anyway. All that I had left was a single man who was the only survivor from the village."

"Tell us how you made him last years, Granmama. Tell us how you cut legs and arms and parts off of him to make the earwig flesh and kept him alive for so long. Tell us how you created flesh from your own body."

"Well, once I realized he was running low on meat and was ready to die, I put his last working part inside my body and forced him to impregnate me. Then I spent the whole next evening with his part in my hand, filling up jars and containers. I cut his throat when his part stopped working and he supplied me with enough flesh to last a few years. It was barbaric, I know, but I had to survive. The world was such a beautiful place, I couldn't let myself die. And I was later able to create people of my own to turn into earwig flesh, my body grew them like a farm."

"Tell us how you kept some of them, Granmama," cry the children. "Tell us how you let some of them grow up."

"Well, I knew I couldn't produce them all myself forever, so I kept a few. Plus I always wanted children I could raise within this beautiful world. Many years later, there was a small community of people here, all of which began from between my legs. Half the people here grow poppy-fruit in the grove behind the village and the other half grow children for the earwig flesh factory."

"Tell us about how your first daughter didn't want to give her children to you. Tell us how you had to start brainwashing your children to do what you wanted. Tell us how you found a poison-plant that messes up people's thoughts."

"No," the old woman says abruptly. "I have work to do now."

"Please, please, please tell us," cry the children.

"No, I need to get to work on the earwig flesh."

"Please, please, please."

"I said *no!*" the old woman screams.

The children lower their heads, pouting again.

Then she points at a small boy. "Billy, it's your turn to get inside of the machine."

The boy groans but nods. He takes the old woman's hand and allows her to guide him to the entryhole of a large black machine. Then he climbs within.

"Give Granmama a kiss," she says to the boy, who pecks her on the cheek and blushes in front of the other children.

The old woman shuts the door and turns on the machine, hurrying to the other side to add bottles of green and pink fluid to the meat.

"Tell us a story, Granmama, tell us a story," the other children shout.

"Which one?" the old woman asks with busy fingers.

"Tell us about when the world changed, Granmama. Tell us about the beautiful ugliness."

The old woman looks at them and smiles at their beautiful goblin faces.

She says to them, "It all started when the night sneezed on the world . . ."

A
SOULLESS MAN

The carpet consists of millions of tiny people. Stepping down on them from my bedside, squishing some between my toes. It's not an easy thing to have a miniature civilization for carpeting. It must be even less of an easy thing to *be* carpeting, especially when the walker above is one as clumsy and ill-eyed as myself. I mash-tread to the mirror, jelly-meat builds and decides to take up residence beneath my heels.

And getting to the mirror, I stare into myself: shaved head, fist tattoo on the chest there, unhealed lacerations from pubescence, and the empty canister where the soul should've been.

These days we keep our souls in little jars. If we do not, the green wind will sweep down from blackness sky and drink it right out of us. Before, we used the organ that pumps blood, which we were born with, but its defense against green wind was inefficient. Wind can pass through organ tissue.

I am one of those victims whose soul-jar broke open, leaving it helpless. And the wind plunged upon me, sucking my essence away, leaving me with a thin layer of emotion resin. I have enough lifeforce to keep me moving, but not enough to bring me happiness, love, hate, or sadness. I am like a whisper that will not go away.

"This is it," I say to the mirror image. "Today will be the day I die."

I don't bother with clothes. I came into this world naked, so I might as well leave it the same.

"I think I'll die in the fresh air, out in the streets." I fake-smile at the mirror. "Most people die in the streets. Why shouldn't I conform to the commonplace for getting killed?"

I feed my pets for the last time. A mouse goes to President Kennedy and some crickets to Presidents Nixon and Ulysses S. Grant. They aren't very friendly pets, sitting numb-eyed bored, and biting me if I touch them.

"I need something to eat too," I tell those who ignore me.

So I go to the kitchen, all wood-rot. Dishes in piles, skank-lanking on the counter. Old food scribbling across the wood. *Sick-sick*, I am thinking.

"How about some Marshmallow Maties and thick milk?" I ask the dining room table, but it doesn't respond because it doesn't like to eat cereal.

After a few bites of chewy-stale mellows, I pour the sog-sloppy slush into the crispy-clogged garbage hole. Then I persuade myself to a warm shower charactered with steam, not using soap or shampoo. Soap can ruin a good shower if you're not skilled at the soap-on-a-rope technique.

I'd say that the best things in life are eating, sleeping, and showering. They are simple things, but easy and the only activities I find satisfying. I'm going to miss those things once I'm dead. Hopefully, people still shower on the other side, if there is an other side. With my luck, the other side will be just as bald-boring as my life is now, or maybe it will be worse. I hope it's not utter perfection, so clean that nobody gets dirty enough to shower, or nobody gets hungry enough to eat, or tired enough to sleep. Some people say that heaven is like that, but it doesn't sound like a paradise to me. I wonder if they'll even let me in now that my soul has been taken away.

I let the shower massage my lizard-spine and neck for an almost-hour, far after my hands prune to nerveless. Tin bathtub, cold-metal taste in my mouth while whistling, and the curtain is a wool comforter that soaks in water to create an old grandpa smell. Once the forced-rain stops, I put on some of that new cologne that you drink to make you sweat sweet odor. And I shave.

A person should look nice when they die. That's what my mother told me. She made sure to look extra nice when she died.

The razor I shave with is keen-straight. Older Brother gave it to me when I grew my first beard, the only present I ever got from him, and it was supposed to be a hint. My first name was engraved on the razor's handle, all five letters in suave stylings. I liked it enough to shave my beard.

Leaving the apartment with the razor as company, breathing cold-dry air. The sun tries to shine, wheezing in fog. Green culture dwelling above me makes the light dim. They are aliens, I'm pretty sure. Either from another planet or from another dimension. Nobody is sure why another civilization would decide to move into our sky, transparent buildings and streets up there. They are blocking out our sun, depressing those who still have soul for it, killing our world. But we can't do anything about them, you know. We are flesh and they are made of gas. It would be like trying to disperse a shadow.

Some say the gases are composed of compressed emotions, and so the sky people need lifeforce in order to build their homes and make babies—which is why they send the green wind after us. That would mean that somebody took my soul away so that he could add an extension to his house. I'm not sure about that theory. I like to believe they are more diabolical than that, like they *feed* on souls, diving down on their prey like spiders from webs.

Strings of white up in green sky. Yes, it appears to be a web from down here. They say if you were to fly through their sky-world it would be like an abstraction of downtown, ghosts in the clouds. I thought it would be an interesting thing to see first-hand before, but I don't care now. I don't care for anything that isn't calm with hushed tones, hopefully the afterlife will be like that.

Walking naked. People stare at me, cringing, amazed at my boldness. It's natural for people to find the naked body wrench-disgusting when in public places, even though it is Man in his natural form. Nobody cries out to the authorities, just ogling at the flab-hairy guy with the razor. My feet slice on the glass asphalt, gouging blood like paint, red footprints trail behind.

"Look at the naked guy," somebody yells from behind. Some laughter follows.

Footsteps approach. Sigh, getting harassed for being naked in public is not the best way to spend my dying moments. Good thing I do not have breasts and a vagina. I would've been destined to get harassing crowds of horny old men, maybe even rapists. Actually, I am not totally safe from rape now. There is a chance some large man might find my body tempting enough to violate. That would definitely not make my day right there. Well, if there is a large homosexual rapist on my encounter list, I'll make sure to cut my wrists quick. Or would it be easier to slash my jugular?

"Hey, naked guy," the male voice says, coming closer to pester me or rape me.

I try to avoid confrontation, crossing the road to a pizza shop that makes a mean three sausage and potato pizza for five bucks on Sundays. Too bad I have no money with me. Too bad it is not Sunday.

The man yells, "You forgot your clothes, flip."

I turn to see him stomping forward, crossing the street. He's a young man, maybe twenty-seven like I, with an orange beard, dirt shirt, and teeny glass-lenses. His soul-container seems fine fit, holding his soul in nicely. A flower painted on the outside.

"You forgot your clothes," he repeats.

"I'm naked on purpose," I say in my stale voice. "I didn't forget."

"You're crazy, flip." He just chuckles there, jolting his head.

The street corner is hammered full with trash. All the garbage pieces cluttered together in a pile, smoking cigarette butts and inhaling gold paint from a spray can—coating their noses with gold chips, and sometimes making them violent.

"What you doin' naked out here, flip?" Eyebrows curl wicked.

"Figured I'd kill myself outside instead of locked up in my apartment," I tell him. "I never wanted to die someplace terribly familiar."

"Wait," Orange Beard says. "You say you're gonna kill yourself?"

"That's right."

Orange Beard turns to his company across the street. "Hey Whitey, this crazy flip's about to kill himself."

I get a good look at Whitey across the street. He's a dark-skinned man with a full-moon beard, twenty layers of pink clothing to make him fat. "Bring him over," he says. "I wanna see him do it."

Orange Beard changes to me, "Mind killing yourself over there so we can watch?"

Shrugging, "If you can take being around a naked guy."

"Don't worry about that, flip. I'm naked out here all the time. Mostly when I'm mind-jambled crazy. You ever get a sunburn on your nuts? It hurts to hell when the skin peels, don't it?"

We scamper across the street, which is soft like a waterbed. The other side of the road is where all the street people live. Street people were once called homeless people, but not anymore. They can't be called homeless, because they have a home: the street. The government makes sure there's lots of street people around. They say that it is friendly to have lots of them in public, because you can think of being in public places as being within someone's home. Doesn't that sound more comforting and friendly? Sometimes a street person will invite you to dinner on the sidewalk and you'll talk politics and philosophy all night long. It is not very good food, but you appreciate their courtesy.

"What's it doing, naked guy?" Whitey says as we arrive to him. I shrug and he goes to Orange Beard. "Hey, did you get any of that koot last night?"

"Na-na," he responds. "She didn't drink enough."

"That's a bitch." Whitey flicks a butt. "Say next week. You'll get the pot, bet?"

"Don't know, flip. Don't know."

I see that Whitey has a civilization of miniature people for a beard, as I have them for carpeting. Replacing anything with a miniature civilization is definitely the sign of a low-class citizen. His beard seems to be white, kind of, but I'm not sure if that's why they call him *Whitey*.

Soon, Whitey sees me staring at him, and gives a dirty look. Staring is a way of insult to street people. They don't like it at all. He lets me slide though. It is my last day alive, so I am entitled to do whatever I want.

Whitey to me, "Hey, naked. Pull up a slab of concrete and sit down."

"Sure," I say, smacking my blubber-bags onto the sidewalk. Scrape-grains rub them red. Then I ask, "Why do they call you *Whitey*?"

Whitey looks at me and toothless-grins. "Because I'm black. Get it? It's a joke."

"How can you call yourself black?" My face goes wrinkled to him. "There aren't anymore black people."

"Well, *I'm* black. My parents made extra sure that I would come out black with none of their white or Japanese blood. They were gene-scientists."

I almost-laugh at him. He does actually look black, but there's no such thing as scientists that can separate mixed genes. And if there was, the government would've had them arrested.

You see, the government was trying to stop racism completely. Equal rights and other such justices weren't helping any, and the number of hate crimes were increasing every day. So the government had to do something rash: they outlawed reproduction between members of the same race. Which means, if you want to have kids you must have them with the person you've claimed an enemy for so long. This was to ensure that nobody would be fully white or black or Hispanic or Asian or whatever after a few generations. It worked too.

These days you can't tell what anyone is. Everyone is kind of a grayish color. I'm not sure about all of the nationalities that make me up, but the ones I know are: German, Chinese, Indian, South African, Irish, Cuban, and Israeli. Of course, most people objected to this law. They said that they would lose their culture if it was mixed in with all of the others. But the government said, "You all had the chance to get along before, and you blew it."

"This is your last day, flip," Orange Beard says to me. "You gotta relax, sauce it easy." He pulls an unlabeled bottle of whiskey from his pants. "Let's celebrate."

I fake-smile, breathing the blister-fluid as he hands it to me. "Whiskey for breakfast, eh?" Then I chug three shots worth, piercing.

"When do you want to kill yourself, flip?" Orange Beard asks.

"I don't know . . . *Now*."

"No, no, no. You gotta get your buzz on first. Everything's better with a buzz. Even killing yourself, I bet."

"Well, I'm getting cold. I was only planning on sitting out here long enough to kill myself."

"Drink some more whiskey, it'll warm you up. Once the bottle's kaput you can put on your show."

I grab the bottle and bring the bottom to green sky. Back in high school, I could drink an entire vodka fifth in one sip. I was like a sort of legend. It's possible to drink hard liquor like water if your throat is callused from yelling or singing all the time. My singing was of the evil-screeching style, so I could drink quite adequately. I now only make it through a third of the bottle though, because I haven't evil-screeched in years.

They are impressed anyway. "Damn, you can drink," says Whitey.

"Yeah. You gotta hang with us more."

"No, I think I'm just going to kill myself now."

"The bottle's not done yet."

I drink into the liquor again, attempting to finish the whole thing so I can get on with killing myself. But I can't empty it, drinking less than the last chug. And the pavement has frozen my buttside numb. Gagging, the whiskey burns up my throat.

"You still got time, naked," says Orange Beard. "You still got time."

Sobriety leaves my body just as my soul did. Maybe it is floating up to the sky-world to mingle with the digested essence. I'm sure I'll never see my sobriety again. I'm buzzed enough now to follow the two street people around town, forgetting all about the cold and the fact that I am naked and the fact that I am supposed to be committing self-murder.

Their daily routine: go to the bakery for stale donuts, go to a corner mart and harass customers until the clerk gives free whiskey, then to the park.

At the park, we get paid for staggering aimlessly and sleeping with newspaper. It's a government job. You see, the government felt so bad for turning so many average citizens into street people that they created jobs for them. The job we are doing is called a *drinking job*, in which we get extremely drunk and wobble-walk about the grass, mumbling lunacy. We are the park entertainers, in other words. And it pays five dollars.

I go in and out of consciousness, dizzy-rolling eyes. I must be an interesting sight to the higher class, being naked and all. The park glows full of green dim-light, children playing with a rubber ball, and older couples observing their wrinkle-reflections in the lake. My legs refuse to stand me up and I find myself sway-sleeping on one of the cold-metal benches for an hour or three. Too tired to kill myself.

Awaking, I see a pleasant face standing over me. A street woman, young and smirking. Above me like an angel from the clouds. Not the green clouds that we have now, but the old clouds. I would've been madly attracted to her if it were the past, but I'm not so sure now. Without a soul, you don't have much of a sex drive.

"You're brilliant," she says in a cute voice, feminine yet deep and raspy.

A *huh?* face becomes me.

"Walking naked in public to prove your liveliness. What a *crazy* way to go."

Her hair is flat-chopped and dirty blue, warm clothes and natural smile. I'm not sure what she is talking about, but I'm guessing it has something to do with the mentality of street people. They believe that craziness is a way to prove strength. She probably has mistaken me for someone trying out insanity by taking to public naked.

"Do you want to go to a party with me?" she asks. "The underground is throwing one of their surrender-the-world bashes."

"I don't think so. I was just about to kill myself."

She makes a *wow* face, thinking that suicide is another

attempt at lunacy. And she shakes her head with glee, happy she's met someone as soul-filled as I.

She tells me, "If you don't kill yourself until after the party, I promise I'll sleep with you."

And I shrug an *okay*, topsy from drink.

Not sure why sex persuades me to prolong suicide, but I think it is because I haven't had any for so long. I won't (can't) enjoy it, but it is something that I should do for memory's sake, just in case they don't have sex on the other side.

When she said the party was an *underground* party, she meant it in the literal sense. The underground is where the street people live when the streets get too cold. It is a maze of sewers and basements and bomb shelters that the street people claimed for themselves.

The girl's name is *Holy*. She says the guys gave it to her because she looks like something from heaven. I almost-laugh at that one. Her hips are rather pudgy-round and the rest of her is slender, creating a distortion in body shape. But I can slightly accept the heaven aspect of her because of her face— red-brown complexion with character-friendly eyebrows and a mouth that is twice the size of mine. If I still had soul for it I would be all over her right now. But I am growing tiresome instead, the alcohol displeasures trying to kick in already. Of course, I still plan on sleeping with her.

"Here we are," she says to me as we enter the main hall of the underworld.

My first impression of it: Fast colors jumbled in a festival, fierce reds, yellows, blues, balconies four levels down with banners of spider-dancing art, river movement in the crowd below, hopping happy people, drinking ones, intimate ones, insanity, screaming. The intensities go far beyond comprehension to my murmur-soul. So much that I almost go swaying off balance. Above ground, it is so gray with the dull-green sky being action at its peak. This is where all of the colors of the world went to, where all the emotion hides.

"Come on," she says. "You have a ticket to the bottom."

I've heard about the social classes of the street people. There are four of them. As she leads me down a great violet-powered staircase, I get to see all four classes in decreasing order. The first class is considered the nethermost class, because it is closer to society. They aren't allowed lower than the top level of underground. You can see why there are levels though. The further I descend, the more life bursts upon me, emitting from the people who reside there. Above ground, the amount of money is what separates the classes. Here, it is the amount of soul. I feel *envious* of these people. They are so below modern society, yet so above it.

I see Orange Beard and Whitey in the third-class section. They chortle and wave, surprised to see me still alive, but I can't speak to them as I advance to the fourth basement. They don't have enough liveliness to go down this far.

"This is where *you* belong," she says as we arrive to the lowest level. Every inch is pure art here, decorated with craziness-colors. I almost go sick at this amplitude of life.

Holy catches the attention of the small crowd of fourth-class partygoers, and introduces me. "This guy is even below *us*. There should be a fifth level for him." She grin-glances at me, kisses me like I am her boyfriend or someone she's known for years. "He is so out there with soul that he walks naked with the society people." Her voice snake-hisses as she speaks of me. Yes, that's what she is—a snake woman. "And he is going to kill himself just to bring disgust into the world's eyes."

The crowd gawks at me, expecting a speech. I shift away, to a wall-sketching so that nobody notices my broken soul-jar. And Holy comments, "There he goes. The artist taking to the art."

The painting is of a man bending over another man who is bending over a third man. I think the point of it is to be crude, but I'm not sure. It does not give me the disgust I feel the artist is trying to give me.

Suddenly, my stomach overturns. I try to ignore it. The pain becomes strident. I drank like a pirate without eating much, now comes the consequences. And I have no choice but to squeeze my stomach, and let it all out. My mouth opens wide, throat tensing, a couple coughs. Then used whiskey protrudes onto the painting in the wall, brown splatters washing down, taking some of the artwork with it.

Almost-cringing, I await for the crowd of emotion people to attack me, maybe the artist will fight me. But instead: *applause.* They clap at my artistic vomit as it slides so beautifully down the wall. Wiping my sour mouth, I try to apologize, but they will have none of that. I am their hero for the night.

"I think I'm going to kill myself now," I tell them, trying to escape the situation.

"Come on," Holy says. "We still have the whole night ahead of us."

I grab her by stiff shoulders. "I'm sorry, but I should be off."

"No," she says. "You haven't even seen my room yet."

Shaking my head with an *I'm way too sick* face, but she ignores my plea, seizing my wrist and pulling me from the crowd. To her room—a hole in the wall, like a cave-closet. She pushes aside the red metal-bead curtain, and lures me inside. A curving motion with her stomach and back. The room is teeming with collectibles, pieces of trash collected from various parts of the city, going to be used for works of art I'm sure. I look down at my razor. Maybe I should cut my wrists now so I can die during sex. I wonder if she would continue with my corpse. Coming closer, her smile-eyes twinkle into my foggy dim ones, wrapping herself around my waist.

Love is free under the city. They don't let social boundaries get in the way. Up there, Holy would've been classified as a *slut*, but down here she is a *queen*, because her love is so active and intense. I've hardly spoken a word to her and she wants some of me already. She thinks I am like her, filled with life and passion. Illusion covers these people like an epidermis. Of course, there is no such thing as an illusionless person, but these people go too far. Everybody has sheets over their eyes and ears as a way to cope with their futures, to make the present more enjoyable.

Holy kisses the corner of my mouth, rubbing the gritty texture on my lower back. The grains discomfort me as she strokes her palm across, digging her nails into my lower mounds gives me satisfaction, but only for scratching an itch. Then she licks the creek of my lips, irritating. I feel nothing. No pleasure. No lust. Just the deepening nausea from whiskey-fumes rising.

As she presses me closer, strongly, to take me through her breast, our soul-canisters clack together. They create an echoing hum, ring-ringing through the cave-closet.

She leans away, giggling. "Our souls are mixing together."

Her wire-fingers crawl my soul-jar, caressing as if trying to caress my soul. Then her smile sinks into a nervous scowl as her fingers discover the crack hiding on the side, and her eyes bead up to mine. She sees emptiness, no emotion through my windows.

"You're a fucking *apathetic*," she says, eyebrows curling, disturbed.

"I'm sorry, I . . ."

She pushes me with disgust. "I *hate* machines. That's what you are, a *machine*." And she rips the container from my chest, a burst of agony, and blood trickles from two large slits, immediate rivers. It would've killed me if it was attached to my heart, as some soul-jars are. She would've literally been *tearing out my heart*. She spits on the container and batter-flashes it to the concrete, breaking in thirds. And pushes me again.

So I lightning-grab *her* soul-box and clench tight. She becomes agitated, nervous-eyes popping open like I put a gun to her head, trying to wriggle it free. I have her vulnerable. Just a slight struggle could tear the emotions right out.

"Do you want to be like me?" My slow voice does not echo as her whimpers do. She says nothing. "Do you want to be a zombie? Do you want to see everything through stale eyes and live, as you say, a *machine?*"

She twitches a *no*, panic-eyes filling me, and her bony palms strained around my arm, resisting. I have my razor in the other hand and could very easily cut her throat, but she would rather have me do that than take her vitality.

"I was hit in the chest with a baseball bat," I tell her. Shrugging, "I don't even know why. I guess he didn't like the way I looked or something." I loosen my grip on her. "He didn't care about beating the rest of my body. Just wanted to break my soul-jar. To make me empty inside. How would you like it if somebody did that to you?" She cuts her nails into my wrist, tiny specks of blood breathe new air.

I tell her, "I could make you like me if I wanted to. So, so easily. And I wouldn't care, wouldn't feel any remorse at all."

Then I let her go, not in the mood to destroy her. Drop my grasp, with alcohol shooting to my dizzy-brain. I have to lean against a wall to prevent falling over. Glancing away from her.

"You're weak," she says, spitting at me. "You don't even have enough rage to go through with it. I could do whatever I wanted to you and you wouldn't care." She spits again and pushes me, agitating me to show emotion. I express nothing.

"*Machine,*" she calls me.

Then she storms out of the room to the other emotion people. I hear the silencing of the music and hundreds of clamor-whispers mounting. Holy shouts, "He's not one of us. He doesn't even have a soul."

As I'm stepping out, bead-strands brushing my naked shoulders cold, a hundred eyes light up, attacking me with glare. Silence. Revolted by my presence. I feel like I should say something, defend myself, but I'm not going to. I'm just standing here, naked in front of a crowd.

27

"Machine," Holy hisses. She kicks dirt at me, clouding up from the cavern floor.

Then another yells *machine*, and another at me. It becomes a chant, all of them join in coordination, "Machine, machine, machine."

I go to the staircase, begin ascending, slow. *Machine, Machine* buzzing in my hangover-ears. They follow after me, trying to taunt with their chorus. *Machine, machine.* But I don't care, just stepping higher and higher, wiping the crusting blood from my chest. *Machine, machine.* Somebody hits me with a mud-ball, breaking against the back of my neck. I continue without acknowledging it. *Machine, machine.* They sound like a train now, going faster, faster. *Machine, machine.* Even Whitey and Orange Beard join in. *Machine, machine.* Another mud-ball in my back, and another. *Machine, machine.* Somebody shoves me. *Machine, machine.*

I make it to the top of the stairs, *machine, machine*, and turn to them. *Machine, machine*, staring dead-eyed to them crowded before me, across the entire underground. *Machine, machine, machine, machine, machine, machine, machine.* Then I do it.

A loud slit reverberates as I bring the razor across my arm's ankle. And the sound breaks the street people's chant. Silence. Then I cut the other, even louder slice emitting. And the only thing we can hear is the sound of blood leaking onto metal stairs, urinating. I whip my wrists at them, spraying tension across their emotional faces. They can see only coldness in my eyes. Not even wincing as I shower them with my life.

And as I'm turning to leave, abandoning them with red-dripping faces, I try thinking of something meaningful to say to them, something they will remember, something wise that a soulless one would tell an emotional one to scrape some illusion from their eyes. But my mind is blank. I can't think of anything important enough to mention. So I saunter from the underground to the street, weeping a trail of blood as I go.

I stroll through a frosty night street to almost-enjoy my last breaths, shaking, staring up at green sky, letting the blood drip-drip. I am not bitter toward the sky people. It was in their nature to take my emotions from me. Unlike the man with the baseball bat, who did it out of hate. Not because he hated me personally, but because he hated the world. I was just a convenient outlet.

There's a burning building ahead. The flames lonely, reflecting against the cloud city. Approaching casually, drawn to the fiery movement. A crowd in chaos, cry-screaming all around the fire building. Things getting slur-hazy for me, weakness coming close, watching the flames dance before me. People so crazy that they hop up and down, and run from side to side.

On arrival, I find a bloody-shirted little girl, asleep yet awake, wandering zombie-dazed. Her chest-container has been torn off, streams of blood like mine. When I become close enough to feel her emptiness, mixing with the cold emptiness that I issue, she stares through me. Almost-bewildered.

"What happened?" I ask her, softening voice.

She trembles, passion-drained face, pointing to the building. Her soul-container is inside somewhere.

"Don't worry," I tell her. "I'll get it for you."

The other people are frantic enough not to notice the bloody naked man shifting around them, stepping right into the burning building. One man says, "Crazy? You can't go in there," but I don't listen. I could care less, merging with the flames.

Standing in the lobby, letting the heat absorb itself into my numb skin, encompassing power. The smoke forces coughs out, but I don't mind. I hold my breath as long as I can.

Eye-searching the floor for a split second, I see some pieces of charred wood from the ceiling. Then the smoke burns my eyes closed. I go dizzy and ease-tumble to the ground, choking on burnt air. I hold my breath again. Crawling the tile, sweep-creeping my palms across, trying to find it—it has to be here *somewhere*. Struggling.

Panicking, I *must* get it. That poor little girl, probably only seven or eight years old. Digging through ash from the entrance to the stairs, not giving up, trying to hold on, trying to contain the little blood I have left. Keeping myself from fading away. Swinging both arms frantic as the blackness fills my head. And a tear breaks from the corner of my eye, slowly slipping under my right cheek. Slowly, so slowly.

CITY OF NEW YORK

Jack Kerby had no idea that the people in New York didn't have any mouths.

He was expecting to see normal human beings when he arrived at the bus station on 179th Street, the same type of people who were at the bus station in Miami, but these people were all wrong: they didn't have any mouths. No tongues, no lips, no teeth, no opening at all, just smooth skin from the nostrils down.

He was taking gentle steps outside the station, a key poking him in his pocket, stirring up anticipation, walking calm-dead among the mouthless New York citizens who moved like liquid.

The city was loud, blaring lights and cars, but the people were quiet. They sounded like shadows. The only noise they made was a piercing shriek that entered Jack's mind from their eyes, slicing into him like miniature demon-worms eating his brainflesh and the sensitive needle-nerves behind the eyeballs.

He had never been to New York before. People told him it was a wonderful place, but that was all. They failed to mention anything about the piercing-eyed citizens without mouths.

Putting his hand into his pocket, Jack began fondling the key, rubbing it until sweat coated his fingers with a strong metallic smell, raising it to his nostrils and inhaling passionately. His eyes closed, sighing for a few moments, a carnal vision.

There was supposed to be a cab waiting out front for him, but there were no cabs in sight. Not at the bus station, not driving in the street.

"Doesn't New York have cabs?" he said to himself.

Jack Kerby didn't know what to do. He sat down on the sidewalk, knees at chin, squirm-watching the cars driving by. All of them were skeleton white, edged with hissing noises. Some of the mouthless drivers would be staring at him as they passed. Not paying attention to the road, just staring with razorblade eyes.

Then something hit him:

The *cold*.

The street was so icy-stabbing, against both his skin layers and psyche, so dark and slick-bladed. The sky didn't contain any stars, just a blank pitch like it was black construction paper. It seemed to be creeping downward and spying, slithering.

Some insects were crawling on the sidewalk next to him, crawling over the ring on his finger. He coughed down to them. They were millepede-like insects, large as rats, making crispy red noises as they tickled his fingers. And Jack winced as he noticed their backs. They had grotesque designs on their upper spines, each design similar to that of a dead infant human face. The faces all had the same look: cold gray skin, stiff open mouths, crusty holes for eyes. Jack ripped his hand away, staring down at them with a rough ogre face. He took the ring off of his finger and put it into his coat pocket. Then he smacked the pests away from him, slap-brushing them off the sidewalk as they made crinkle-squeals, antennas wiring.

A car pulled up to him, filling his entire view with yellow, and then the cab door opened. Darkness was scurrying within, a murky haze. Jack stood, the pale street lights swarming, reflecting off the slick winter on the street. And he let the cab's darkness embrace him.

Inside, on the hard plastic seats, he watched the driver's eyes piercing into him through the rearview mirror, a silent scream that jerked Jack's vision to the outside. The driver said nothing other than that. He eased into traffic and accelerated to a decent speed.

Jack sat quiet for awhile, watching the ghostly New Yorkers walk like smoke down the icy sidewalks. He didn't know how to respond. They were so foreign to him. He never would have guessed that New York was so outlandish.

"It's pretty cold for September," Jack told the cab driver, breaking the silence with his tic-shivering voice. The cab driver pierced his eyes through the rearview mirror again but said nothing. Jack retreated to the window.

He continued to the silent man, "It doesn't bother me though. I've always had an attraction to the cold." He turned to see the driver's eyes no longer in the mirror, switching his vision back to the funereal street.

"That pretty much explains why I married my wife." Jack's neck tightened, a whistling in his nose that he didn't regard. "Jami is as cold as they come. I knew she wouldn't stay faithful to me the day I married her, everyone knew. Her touch sent a chill up my spine that day, her kiss was like a goldfish swimming into my mouth. But still, I *had* to marry her. I've always been attracted to cold, cold women who treat me like shit."

Jack paused to take the key out of his pocket, examining it, rubbing it tightly with his thumb sweat. "It's not wrong for me to do it, you know? I'm just getting even with her."

The cab stopped in front of a large inn and the driver's eyes reappeared within the mirror. Jack looked into his eyes, shaking his head, "I'm just getting her back."

Jack dug within his wallet and held some bills to the driver. But the driver wasn't moving, his eyes still within the mirror. "Take it," Jack said, but nothing. So Jack sat there for a few minutes before dropping the money on the seat.

Gray icy emotions were still in the air as he exited the vehicle. The cab remained parked there with the engine buzzing, the driver still gawking within the mirror even though his passenger was missing. He didn't leave until Jack reached the entrance, roaring the gas pedal and then screeching away.

The lobby of the inn was bright and deserted. No one was at the front desk, no one walking about, no furniture even. An empty vastness.

Jack could hear his feet crunching the stale carpeting as he went to the staircase and climbed toothpaste steps to the third floor. The key was in his hand, still rubbing metal scent into his fingers. He found the hall of the third floor deserted as well and without carpeting or much light, sandy corners and webby electrical snakes inside the wall holes.

At door 313, paint-splashed stains and splinters across its surface, Jack took a deep breath. He knocked quietly as if scared to disturb the musty atmosphere.

No answer.

So he put the greasy key into the door and walked within. A wrinkled small room with concrete instead of carpet. All barren besides a bed in the center holding piles of blankets and towels and underwear, and a woman sitting within a long sweaty shirt, nipple-pumps poking through the fabric.

They stared into each other. Like the others, she had blank skin where the mouth should have been, sitting there piercing-eyed in his direction.

"I got the key," Jack told her, shutting the door crookedly behind him. "Jami didn't see the envelope. She thinks I'm on a business trip." He didn't come any closer, nervous-skinned. "You should've told me you were going to send it. I'm glad you did, but it was a surprise."

The woman didn't move her body at all, just watching him.

"So you're in New York for the month?" Jack asked.

He tapped the key in his palm.

"Well, how's work?"

No response.

"How's your husband?"

Nothing.

Jack began to pace. He glanced into the crumbling bathroom to see a millepede insect climbing a crack where the mirror should have been. Its infant face droop-staring at him as it wire-crawled. Jack went to the window with disgust, attempting to look out at the big city but the glass was painted over with charcoal, blinding him. He sighed, didn't know what to do.

Then an arm crash-wrapped around his waist from behind that made him jerk, nails digging into his chest, crawling up his shirt into his skin. He turned to her embrace, arms gripping him tight. He didn't hear her get off the bed and creep up to him. She was smooth against his skin, the texture of plastic, no wrinkles or pores. Sliding his body.

When she kissed him, he felt nothing. No wetness. Only a feeling like putting a hand on a shoulder. She was rubbing her mouthless skin against his neck as if to suck, but he felt no sensation. She pulled off her wet shirt, beads of moisture running between her breasts.

"You're beautiful," Jack said, concentrating on her perfect parts rather than her missing mouth. "I didn't think I could meet anyone this beautiful on my computer."

She stole his coat and went for the shirt, ripping at it, but Jack grabbed her rubber hands tight. Her eyes piercing him with anger and frustration, still straining to break the buttons way, touch his skin and make it sweaty like hers. But he got away from her and unbuttoned his shirt carefully. Before finishing, the woman wormed her arms up into his armpits and encircled his gooseflesh, tickle-crawling and pulling him against her slippery chest.

He unzipped his fly while the woman removed his belt. Then Jack looked up at her and jumped. Jerked her hands away, retreating to the bed.

Her nose was gone.

It was missing just like her mouth, a flat featureless face from the eyes down. Her stare was dazed at him, stepping forward to gorge into him. He wondered how she could breathe without nostrils or mouth, she was not suffocating.

Jack shivered as she rubbed her smooth hand through his hair, tension lifting the skin on his eyebrows. But he let her plastic hand explore, let her take down his pants and fondle him, the millepede insect twitching in the bathroom behind her.

He put the woman's face in his hand. Looking in her eyes, he noticed a purple haze within them, drowning his mirror image. She closed her eyelids and nuzzled her cheek against his palm. Jack caressed the woman's pale head and flattening ears. Then her hair began to fall out. Locks dropped into his hand, onto the floor. Jack's heart was pounding, fighting him.

Then she opened her eyes. Her smooth bald head shiny in the dim light. Without breaking eye contact, she slid her underwear off and tossed it to the side, curly hairs exploding as it hit the bed.

"What are you?" Jack asked her, examining the changing woman.

Then she attacked him, took his boxers down, pulled his face into her breasts, tore into his back. Jack closed his eyes and let her fierce-finger him with rubber parts, digging into him, pulling his shoulders apart. When he opened his eyes, he saw the millepede insect was as big as a dog now, twitching on the cracky bathroom wall. Jack closed his eyes again and kissed the woman's bald mouth. He pushed her away before reopening them.

"I can't," he said. "I'm sorry, I can't." She stared deeply, tilting her head from side to side. "I still love her."

The woman rubbed her index finger down Jack's face and pressed herself against him. He shook his head, glancing back at the insect. It had grown again. BIG. It was the size of a horse now, twisting antennas, grease dripping from the dead infant's face. Jack broke from the woman's grip and pulled the bathroom door shut before the giant insect had a chance to squeeze into the room. Muscles on the doorknob, Jack heard the creature attacking the door, wiry limbs emerging from underneath to scrape his ankles.

The woman attacked again from behind, wrapped around him, breaking his grip on the doorknob. And she threw him onto the bed, pinning him down as the insect scream-hissed at the wood barrier. Jack gasped as he saw the woman's face peering down on him. Her eyes were missing now, melted into her flesh. She was faceless, an egg of skin attached to a neck. But she moved as if she could see, mock-licking him with her smooth head. Jack tried getting her off, but was feeling too blur-heady and couldn't overpower her. The atmosphere was getting to him, making him weak and fuzzy. It also aroused him, made him cease the resistance, let her have her way. The woman lifted her plasticky hips so he could enter her. But as she lowered to encompass him, Jack's penis poked a crotch of smooth skin and slid away. She had no holes.

The woman didn't realize this and smeared her blank crotch against him as if he was within, pulsating as the bathroom door squeal-banged and cracked. Jack was too shocked to move, tears hitting his neck. He watched as the girl's hands were being eaten by her wrists, and breasts swallowed by her ribcage. She orgasmed as her head sunk into her neck, her arms folding up into her back. Jack closed his eyes, screaming. The insect's wood-chewing trickled in his ears as his eyes opened to what had become of the woman.

She lay heavy on his stomach, a large oval-egg of meat. No limbs or features. A smooth jittering ball of human being.

His body screamed, rolling the woman-thing off of him and jumping from the bed. He eyed it carefully as he put on his clothes over sticky wetness. New Yorkers are insane, he thought to himself. The insect creature was halfway through the bathroom door by the time Jack left. He watched it breaking away the wood to get at him, but didn't wait around to see what would happen. There was only one thing Jack had left to do. He had to get out of New York.

He rushed down the stairs and into the street, with his vision flickering, charging through the iciness. He realized his mind was not working right. It had not been right ever since he arrived at the bus station, like he was in a memory. Logic was not at all apart of his thought process and did not know how to react to that.

His body froze once it hit a major road. The sidewalks were cluttered with dozens of balls of meat similar to what the woman had become, in all different sizes and shades. They were scattered along the street and in broken cars beside the road. Jack looked up to the nearby buildings, picturing everyone in New York as ovals of flesh, lying in their beds, on their couches in front of televisions, submerged in bathtub water.

Then he noticed the insects in the distance, large millepede-creatures coming out of manholes like ants, collecting the balls of meat with large pincher jaws and carrying them down into the sewers one by one, to their nests.

Jack ran. He didn't know where to go, but he ran. Straight for the closest building which happened to be a pool hall, charging at it with stumbling sloppiness. But before reaching it, a manhole opened up to a hissing millepede in his path, a dead baby mouth moaning at him. Jack fell backwards as it turned and screamed in his face. The scream sprayed a numbing gas, and he felt something slide down his throat. The gas hit his nerves so hard that he jerked his legs in response, kicking the insect in a large jelly eye. It shrieked and ducked into the sewers, giving Jack some time for escape.

The door of the pool hall burst open and Jack plowed within, his nerves scrambled and heavy. Within, there was a crowd of flesh balls, on bar stools and benches. He felt his body draining and making him fuzz-drunk.

"Poison," he said to himself, wiping the insect venom from his lips.

He staggered around pool tables to the bathroom in the corner, crashing through the door and sliding down a wall to bitter cold tiles, tears burning in his eyes, muscles relaxing.

Before his heart had a chance to calm, it was jerked to tension as he heard some squeaking within one of the stalls. He pulled himself up, drug-dizzy spins as he stepped to the door. It was locked. The shrill tightened his eardrum, creating acid-swirlings within his reeling thoughts. His eyes faded closed, then reopened. He drifted to his hands and knees, and looked underneath the stall door. As he peered up, he saw another human ball of flesh on top of the toilet seat. But it was discolored, greenish-gray and sand-textured, much older than the others. A strong scent like burned liver crept up Jack's nostrils as he crawled into the stall and stood, peering down at the ball to see the top missing with a little squeaking millepede within.

Jack squirmed uncomfortably as it chewed on the flesh and devoured the egg from the inside out. He reclined against the stall door and watched it feed for awhile, watched it clean the meat off the thin half-melted bones with sharp perfection. His head rolled back and forth at it, shifting the hazy sensations from one side of his brain to the other, blinking.

Eventually, Jack unlocked the stall door and left the pool hall. He picked up a paper at a nearby newsstand and strolled down the lonely sidewalk towards the bus station, passing a meteor crater the size of a football field and rubbing his eyes languidly as he tried to read the blurry newsprint.

His lips were melting together, but he didn't seem to notice.

Fist World

Jesus Christ finds the process of going to the bathroom exhilarating.

He didn't before his crucifixion, mind you, when going to the bathroom was far-far from pleasurable and toilet paper did not consist of soft-softness as it does today, if there was any toilet paper at all back then. Was there? No, I think they would just use shreds of vegetation, or their sleeve, or possibly the skin of lower class citizens. No, Jesus didn't enjoy it in those days one itty bit. And if the Jesus Christ didn't enjoy it, you could imagine how bad it was for all the non-messiahs. Or did Jesus perform a miracle when going to the bathroom? Maybe God would come down and clean his soiled bottom with heavenly cloth so that Jesus would not scrape himself on anything uncomfortable. Maybe this was why everyone during that era was so irritable besides Jesus and his followers. But who really knows? The authors of the bible didn't mention anything of the sort. Or did they? No, I'm pretty sure they'd send you to the lions for taking interest in that sort of thing. Perversions were probably illegal. Does this mean that Jesus is a pervert? Well, it is quite strange how the son of God is fascinated by bathroom activities, but I don't want to call him a pervert.

Now that he's dead, Jesus can spy on you all he wants while

you are unaware. It is not a sin to be a peeping tom when you are a ghost, so he does not think twice about it. However, there are some people (like me) who know all about his little game and are scared to go to the bathroom because of it.

I sense him in the bathroom with me right now, his raping eyes from behind or below me. I try to ignore him, stare-locked at the splinter-wood wall, my bare toes rubbing against the moist-smoothed surface of an apple core, covering my pubic hairs and gritty shank. I know he's around. The guy at the gas station told me—the guy with the metal-wire beard and the six-inch nails for eyes. He works down there in his dust-croaked suit and talks all about how Jesus, the dead messiah, haunts my home.

Sometimes I will go down there for gas and he will not let me leave until I pet his dog that has mutated into a fish-like thing. He keeps it in a refrigerator that is on its back filled with green water, grit-slimy gravel on the bottom, and it smells a lot like sausage gravy. The fish/dog flaps thin tentacles that protrude from its belly, wiggling them throughout the thick liquid like they are keeping it afloat. It cannot bark anymore, but sometimes it will let out a growl, a bubbling of water and a deep rumble through the sides of the refrigerator. The gas station man is proud of his pet, admiring it with his twisting eyes and soggy grins. He brings my palm to its scaly back sometimes and rubs it along the globby hairs or some tentacles. I always cringe and pretend I am back home.

He tells me, "You know, Jesus Christ is staring at you from the bottom of the toilet water while you are sitting there, looking up at your feces as it creeps slowly out of you."

I just nod and try not to smell his seaweed/anchovy breaths, or look directly into his pointy eyes. He says he can see things very keenly with his eyes. He can even see the ghosts that wander our world between dimensions, even Jesus' ghost. He says Jesus has dark skin, bushy eyebrows, and a crooked nose. He says that he keeps to himself mostly, hardly ever seen walking with any of the other ghosts. "They don't seem interested in the messiah. Maybe they are disappointed that he is not as great as the bible says."

I wipe myself and pull my pants up really quick. I stare into the toilet to see if his reflection is shimmering in the water there. Nothing. Not even a crucifix. I flush it away, click-swirling down. If he had been there, his spirit would have been pulled through millions of plastic pipes across the landscape and into a monster septic tank that lives over the gloom-bitter mountain. He'd have to walk all day and most of the night to get back here. He probably wouldn't even bother.

I know I wouldn't bother. I've taken that hard blistering journey over the mountain, to the city of black machines that growl and sweat high into the cloud world, miles of motion, coughing churning, scream-steaming, a monster train that never departs. The walk is so long that your eyeballs puss over before you arrive, a greasy film that hazes you. Your pores bleed, your whole body shivers with weakness, and the thin windy air seems to sweep away strips of your skin.

Sometimes I'll go there to make sure the beasts are not broken down. Just making sure. I always shake my head once I get there, sit down, gasping, shaking my head. It's like checking to make sure the sky is still in the air. Such a long walk to prove myself an idiot. I usually contemplate putting my head into the teeth of one of those hungry beasts, allowing it to tear through my neck and unfold the skull into strings of red meat. But I never do it. The thought of meeting Jesus' ghost after my death continuously alters my suicide plans.

I step out of the bathroom, hoping Jesus isn't stalking behind me, to the droopy frizzle-crinky room which is the rest of my house. It squeezes around me, creeps its closeness into the pit of my brain.

I leave. Dart out of the door to the front porch, and it gives a sigh as I sit into it, ooze into the log made rocking chair. A splinter bites my thigh, but I allow it. The relaxation is pleasing, decent. A bottle of watermelon juice goes straight to my lips as I dream of a beautiful truck driver and her slender-curvy flesh parts.

My eyes go into the landscape:

Bland fields stretching miles in the black-grass valley. They are beneath a pink-speckled quivering sky, which seems to hang a little too close above me, like I am finely printed words that it is trying to read.

The fields grow a single year-round crop: hands.

Human beings have evolved to a point where hands are like the tails of lizards, just a little jerk in the right nerve and they pop off at the wrist. Just like that. But unlike the tails of lizards, human hands do not grow back. Evolution is strange how it goes sometimes. One day a man will make a living as a professional boxer, and the next his hands are falling off from doing too many pullups. It is quite irritating, even dangerous at times. But you can get new hands for a small amount of money. They sell them at supermarkets everywhere in the bigcity, right between the creamed socks and pickled candles, and the supermarkets get them from hand farmers like me.

The truck driver comes every other Thursday and picks up a load. She always smiles at me when she comes with BIG green-painted lips, twirling locks of her crazy-grass hair.

"They're always in demand," she says, but I hardly hear her. I am too busy picturing the two of us on a stroll in the fields, wrapped around each other without talk, or I think of awaking one night to find her in my bed, on top of me, channeling through my insides with her cherry eyeballs.

She doesn't talk to me about the bigcity, not even when I ask. I haven't seen it in years and wish she would take me there with her, see what has become of it, but she never tells me. I'm not sure it exists anymore.

Supposedly, there have been many changes. The man at the gas station says that beings from Saturn live among us now. He says they came in a ship resembling a dollar bill and now fill up ghettos along the west coast. I never talk to the gas station man. He tells me things, but I never tell him things. He is the only person for miles and I still don't tell him things. He tells me how the world has gone flat again, how people decided not to like Columbus anymore and so they cut the surface off the planet and flattened it out. It orbits the sun like a piece of paper these days, just beside the bald sphere. I am confused about which one we call Earth. When I dig, I am scared that I might go too far and create a BIG hole in the planet. I might even fall through and go tumbling forever.

I ask the truck driver if what the gas station man says is true and she smiles at me and blows bubbles with her raisin-flavored chewing gum. She is so exquisite with her looks, but she sometimes reminds me of an endless flight of stairs. That's what the gas station man calls me: an endless flight of stairs.

I wish the truck driver was here with me right now. She always cheers me up with her smile and eyeballs. She told me she would come early this week, but she has yet to show. I hope I have the courage to ask her to eat dinner with me this time. I have been planning out what I will say and have cleaned my house too. Well, mostly. Maybe I will just wait until next week.

I open a book. It is BIG and has lots of words in it. I take a chewed pen to it and draw a square around a paragraph. I color it in, ripping the paper slightly, and put flowers around the sides. I draw the sun with a scraggy beard and ears. I sometimes try putting in the truck driver, but I can never draw her as beautiful as she really is. Actually, I can't even draw her to look human. The gas station man says that the ghosts don't like my drawings. They think my art looks childish and he makes me so mad that I run away from him and throw rocks at plants.

However, I can draw parts of the truck driver. Her hair especially. I swirl lines on the page to and it looks just like her wild hair, and I can almost see her eyes underneath those hairs winking at me.

Then I notice a breath hitting the back of my neck.

I pause.

I don't turn around, joints stiff. Jesus Christ must be behind me. He's probably trying to look down my shirt to see my chest hairs.

I ignore him and continue with drawing. Cautiously, nerves twitching in my collar bone, I adjust my shirt flat to blind him from my torso skin. Immediately, I sense his disappointment in the air.

Looking to the distant mountain that blocks the machine world from visibility, I become inspired. I decide to draw it next to the truck driver's hair on the bundle of words, smiling and sipping watermelon juice as I go, thinking about drawing the machines on the next page.

"The machines run the world," the gas station man says. He told me that they control the weather and the temperature of the planet. He also said that they control gravity and if the machines ever break down, we will float off the planet into space. The world would end if we didn't have them. Sometimes I get so worried about the machines breaking down that I can't sleep at night. I have to go check up on them. Take that long walk across the plain to see if they are okay.

I shriek as a breeze flushes through my pant leg, quickly slapping it shut. It must have been Jesus trying to feel up my leg. Jerk-standing, dropping my book to the dirt, I go into the fields to pace.

The man at the gas station says that sometimes Jesus is physically attracted to men, but is not actually gay. He will kiss you on the lips, but not in a sexual manner. Jesus is above sex. Or is Jesus sexually confused? I cover my mouth, just in case. I couldn't imagine having the savior's tongue slip into my lips when I am unaware.

I stomp my bare feet through rows of hands growing from

the soil. The hands are almost fully ripe now. They are tight fists, raised in pride or maybe anger, thousands of them roaring, a crowd to a tyrant. Stampering the field, not turning around to my ugliness-home, knowing Jesus Christ is behind me.

The sky sinks lower, just a short distance from my head. It is trying to crush me, suffocate me. The man at the gas station says that the sky used to be a giant ocean, but the water got stretched out for miles-miles wide/high until it became a gas. He also says that someday it will compress back into an ocean and drown us all. I look up a lot these days.

I kick a growing fist off of its roots, then stomp it into the soil until I separate some fingers with my heel. My lungs break down to harsh whispers. I pause. My eyes go forward, imagining Jesus Christ masturbating with one of the hands in front of me, probably fantasizing my image as he does it. My throat goes sick, tendons stretching the neck skin.

I run away. Out of the field, down the road that knows the gas station and the highway. I don't go quickly, my bare feet slicing against the sharp gravel, blood trickling, a bruise under a toenail.

Rocks crash-scurry behind me, sounding as if coming to hit me. I think Jesus is throwing them, angered that I am leaving him. I don't turn around, moving faster despite the feet suffering. The noises continue, clinking rocks against one another behind me. I keep moving until the noise fades, Jesus giving up.

Ten minutes.

I find myself at the gas station and freeze.

Look back.

My house has disappeared from my sight, only a line of field can be seen from this distance. I turn to the gas station, then back to my house. Which is the lesser of two evils? The perverted ghost of Christ or the man with the mutated dog? I choose the gas station man, hiking up to his tiny shack at the highway.

All along the sides of the road, I see white-painted animals frozen-posed at random. The gas station man enjoys capturing small animals and spray painting them until they go hard, then he places them around the outside of his house like lawn ornaments. They can be found all over the highway: rabbits, lizards, birds. It is his hobby. He is a very decorative man.

I approach him from behind as he empties gasoline onto the pavement and highway, his red flannel shirt flickering in the shatter-breeze. My sight goes to the street, down the wavy worm to the mountains, huge blues bulging from thunderclouds. The sky seems to be popping in places, sizzling, churkling, like it has a short circuit somewhere.

The gas station man hears me coming. "I haven't seen you in awhile," he says to me.

"I've been busy," I say, staring at the gas splashing on the street, but my voice was mumbled and he probably didn't hear me.

"Doing what? Watching the fists grow around you?"

I nod and look at the horizon that meets the road. It is purple and marble-swirly, whispering.

"Is Jesus behind me?" I ask, soft-trembling.

He turns to me with his needle eye-spins, clicking sounds, and looks over my shoulder, piercing into the other world. Then he goes back to his work.

"No," he answers. "There's no one behind you." He bites at a bumblebee circle-flying the gas stream. "Is Jesus bothering you?"

"The whole world is bothering me." My voice surprisingly loud.

"You know what I do when something is bothering me?" he asks.

I look at the dirt under my fingernails.

"That's right," he said. "I get rid of it."

A breeze scurry-swarms under my skin, nerves crawling, ticking.

"See," says the gas station man, "this highway's been giving me trouble lately. No one ever drives it anymore. I'm gettin' put out of business." He spits an oil-goo at my feet. "So I've decided to burn it down."

I nod at him, wandering my eyes across the terrain. I see a truck parked off the side of the road by the gas station. The truck driver's truck, muddy with a flat tire, black paint on the side with crude designs. But she is nowhere to be found.

"Where is she?" I ask the gas station man.

"Who?"

I clear my throat and speak louder, "The truck driver. Where is she?"

"Her truck broke down," the gas station man says with sincerity, shaking his head.

"Where is she?"

The gas station man's gas stream dies away, so he takes a hose from the next pump and continues.

"She's an interesting girl, isn't she?" he says.

I glance at the blood on my toes.

"Green hair, green lips, blood-red eyes." The gas station man licks his lips within wiry beard hair.

Pressure builds on my eyeballs, fists clenching.

"Blood red eyes," he says, smiling at me and nodding his head. "Bloody, blood red."

He laughs and sprays the gas like a sprinkler.

"What have you done with her?" I crack-scream at him.

The gas station man stares deep at me.

I say, "Where is she?"

Then he jumps, pointing over my shoulder and yelling, "Look, Jesus is behind you!"

I jerk around to see nothing, just open landscape and white animals.

"He's got his hand in your pants!" he screams at me. "Quick, stop him!"

I throw my fists about, lunging away in squeals.

"He's under your shirt! Get him out of there!"

I run, fleeing the ghost. The gas station man is laughing at me as I go. His laugh scrapes the top of the mountain, screeching, driving blood to swell my brain.

Charging into his home, my feet too torn and raw to make it all the way to my own house. I slam the door shut and put my weight against it so that the Jesus ghost will not come inside.

The gas station man continues screeching his laughs from the highway. Through the window, I peek at him walking down the median, emptying a bucket of gas over his shoulders in the distance.

My standing grows tired so I slide down the crumbly door, turning to a tiny room without furniture. It is all white, rough white. A single blanket is on the wood floor in the corner, his bed, and there is a cage of rabbits, prairie dogs, turtles that are ready for spray painting. Under my black toes: wetness. I find a trickle-trail of blood there which leads across the room and disappears underneath a door.

I get to my sour feet—the gas station man's wild laugh persisting—step across the room to the door and open. Another blank white room. I didn't expect the gas station man's home to be so bland.

The blood is sprinkled to another room, also empty, and ends at a manhole in the center of the wood floor. I go to the rim and peer down. Inside of the hole: electric dark. Sparks twitching within. I descend to a crowd of television sets, no, computer screens, all around me. Their faces squeeze me in the shivering black, and as I look upon them, they show me familiar sights. I gasp, nearly fall to the ground.

Fists.

I see thousands of fists. *My* fists. Each computer screen shows a different angle of my field . . . and my porch, my house, *inside* my house.

I hold my breath inside of me, trying to calm. There have

been little cameras hiding around my property this whole time, hiding within fists and within cracks of wood. Spying, keeping an eye on me.

From across the darkness, a splash of electricity lights the corner, sparks popping, blistering. Then a woman's cry bursting at me. It whines for a moment, then slides away.

I step closer, my eyes focusing into the dimness. A figure stands there, squirming, tied up maybe.

"What has he been doing to you?" I say.

It cries again, her voice gurgling, trying to form words.

When I step closer, I recognize a large sheet of glass separates us. A window.

"I'll get you out," I tell her, grabbing a computer and spinning it around to shine light on the glass, and she brightens.

The truck driver is naked in front of me, white skin swollen behind the glass, floating. She is in water, submerged within a tank of water. Her green hair waving in the thick liquid, green lips open to me. All of her is green now, tinted skin, turning scale-slimy. Tentacles are growing from her stomach and breasts, snaking through the fluid, just like the gas station man's dog. She is attached at the belly to a large cord, connected to a black machine beside her water tank.

A jolt of electricity hits her again, sparks flame-showering from the machine. She erupts from the water gargle-splashing, squawking at the pain, her naked body rubbing against the glass. Our eyes meet, her cherry-red eyes glowing into mine as she gasps for air, but nothing enters her lungs.

She fades down into the liquid, still gleaming into my eyes. Gills open up on her neck to breathe the water's air. Staring, just staring at me. Then she closes her eyes and feigns sleep. The tentacles flutter her until she turns around to expose a thin lump growing down her back, preparing to be a large ugly fin. My face contorts with disgust.

I explode from the house and into the red-smoky landscape. The highway is on fire. From horizon to horizon, the long highway has been set ablaze, demons dancing across the wind. I yell at it, rage at it, but it overpowers me, squeezes me into a ball.

I go to the gas station man's tool shed, fighting off the color red, screaming. I rip open the door and find a pickax under a wheelbarrow, then tear it out of the mess.

My hand falls off. It pops off at the wrist as the pickax catches on a hose, and now it twitches spidery on the ground. I grab the fallen member with the surviving hand and toss it at the fire-highway, screaming redness, pounding my forehead into the metal shed.

I look for the gas station man, but I am alone. My second hand carefully pulls the pickax from the hose-knots and rests it on my shoulder, and I scan the landscape for him, screaming his name, craving to put him in a tank of electric water until he turns into a fish.

The demons within the wind open tar-mouths at me, moaning for escape as if prisoners within the smoke. My mind is chaotic, searching for the gas station man with sharp jerks of my vision.

There he is:

A bundle of blackness within the flames, burning like a tire. I run up to him, swinging the pickax inside the flames to get at him, but I cannot reach. The smoke burns my eyes closed and forces me back.

"Why?" I yell at the gas station man, tear-frustrated that I cannot hurt him. "Why, why, why?"

And my anger sends me charging away from the highway. I take the road back to my house, the flames following on my left, eating up the crop, running through the crowd of fists raised in my direction. As the fire reaches them, the fists open up to fry and melt. I lace boots onto my swollen feet and fit myself up for a new hand, a strong one that will hold.

The pickax in both of my fists and flames churkle-dancing the horizons, I turn away from the fields and the gas station, still screaming with rage but the screams have grown deeper like growls. And I start the long hike over the mountain. To the land of helpless black machines . . . to get rid of what's been bothering me.

Scrows

They seem 2-dimensional, tiny people resembling blank pieces of paper, paper dolls actually, or gingerbread men without faces. Sometimes they will come down from the ceiling, ooze-slowly as if spiders lowering themselves from the webby string. No expressions on them, just the featureless glare and tarantula movements.

I lie in my bed watching them, their jumping puppet-like walk across the room, their piercing silence as I try to close my eyes to sleep. They never leave me alone when I sleep, they always want to come into bed with me, dance awkwardly on top of my stomach and breasts.

I go into the kitchen to find something to drink and pills to down, and they are there, float-hopping along the tile floor to get to the living room. I step on one as it crosses under my nightgown, grind my bare foot upon its cold paper body, twisting to shred it to bits. But it does not come apart, holding strong. After I release my heel, it pops back up and drifts on cranky, making jerking motions of anger. They can't be killed.

People say they are not dangerous, that they cannot possibly hurt a human being with their weakly little bodies, but there isn't any proof to back that up. You can see how cold they are, how vile their drilling machine-like minds can think. They are disgusting, horrible creatures. They are not the faithful servants of man as first speculated.

I mope to the plexiglass window, my swollen eyes staring into the swarm of black crispy insect bodies, *gargoyle beetles*, pile-squirming the desert landscape. They came a few years ago, popped out from nowhere into existence, a massive infestation that took us by surprise. The beetles reproduce in such a number that their masses cannot be contained, eating the vegetation scarce, spreading a cruel disease. They go by the name of *gargoyle* because they sleep frozen like statues during the day, they don't go underground, just resting in piles along the landscape, basking in the sun. You step on them constantly, crunching through your driveway to get to your car, a couple will buzz into your hair and clutch onto your earrings with crabclaw strength. You'll find them dead in your purse, little stiff shells with crooked-flexed legs. For awhile, people were unable to stay sane because of these numerous pests refusing to keep to themselves. You couldn't sleep at night because dozens of them would be crawling in your bed, you couldn't breath because you were afraid one would fly into your mouth, you couldn't eat without some getting into your food. And there weren't any pesticides that could kill them. They were worse than cockroaches.

Some people became so twitchy that they had to be put on heavy medication so that the crawly insects would not be a bother to them, putting them into humming trances while the gargoyle beetles crept up their limbs and down their shirts.

But then came the *scrows*, the tiny paper doll creatures who were manufactured to rid us pests. They are called scrows as a short form of *scarecrows*, because that's what they are, in a sense: tiny scarecrows that drive away pests. There is a chemical they emit that causes fear in small creatures, and the scrows have an endless supply of it. No matter how much they spray at the beetles, they will never run out.

And so these scrows came to be, little living beings who have their own thoughts and maybe even cultures, reproducing by the dozens. And though the scrows drive the gargoyle pests out of human homes, they are really just pests themselves. Pests with intelligence.

I go to my bathroom and piss while showering. A flood of beetles stare at me through the narrow window above my bruised shoulder, cluttered as a beehive, but I try to look at my feet and ignore. My shoulders and limbs are beaten and swollen. Everyone these days are beaten and swollen, huge black/blue markings covering the skin. They say it is from the disease the gargoyle beetles carry, something that attacks your nerves and weakens you. It is a virus that clubs you, bruises you from within. And it makes you feel constantly dirty, even when in the shower.

Two scrows are at the shower's window, hopping slowly like they are on the moon, spraying their fluid to scare the insects away. However, the fear-toxins do not penetrate the glass. They just make me dizzy and nervous of their movements. I'm sick with agitation.

I suspected bad things from them ever since the first day the delivery men brought them into my home. I could sense it. The scrows came drift-walking in like a wind was carrying them, little mechanical ghosts, and the atmosphere was filled with an uneasiness. The delivery men said it was just the fear-chemical that made them so disturbing to be around. I cringed a dirty look and said, I thought they were invented to make our lives more comfortable?

I leave the shower, drip wetness on a scrow passing by and it becomes irritated, rapid-jerking in circles to threaten me. My naked image appears in the mirror. A wrinkled old woman of twenty-five, covered in bruises. The eyes contain dark bags and the eyeballs are fading of color. The world is falling apart. I can't hold it together at all any longer. I'm so dreadfully tired.

The other day, I was gazing out the window, hoping somebody would stop by for a visit. I was watching the little boy across the road, playing with his little green soldiers on the steps in his yard, surrounded by scrows so the gargoyle beetles would not bother his game. They were hover-jumping about the sidewalk, leaping over the boy's action figures, attacking the beetles with their horrifying spray. The boy wasn't paying attention, making explosion noises and scratching at the large scabs on both knees.

The beetles were too many, piling over the sidewalk in large heaps, trying to get at the boy's sweat. There were more than usual, hundreds, and the scrows were hard at work trying to scare them away.

Then, all of a sudden, the scrows began to slow down. They were running out of juice and dimming to a hazy stance. The gargoyle beetles took the opportunity to flood onto the steps, buzz-swarm on top of the scrows, piling, grasping tiny legs around them. And the scrows were rip-springing, jittery movements. They were confused, deranged, maybe scared. They probably never had the beetles overpower them before, never got taken down to have tiny insects crawl their paper-like figures. They scattered madly, twitching, retreating towards the boy.

I froze warp-eyed when I saw it happen, so quickly and unexpected. A scrow leaped at the boy and took off a large section from his shoulder. There wasn't any blood, the scrow just seemed to absorb a chunk of flesh from him without cutting, like part of his body had just been erased, and the boy's eyes widened stiff, too confused to scream.

Then another scrow jumped at him. It sucked away his entire elbow and the rest of the arm fell to the concrete to get slurped up by some excited little ones. And the scrows were all electrified by their actions, hopping up and down at the boy and absorbing large pieces of his body with every jump.

After only a couple minutes, the boy was completely gone, vanished. And the scrows went back to spraying fear into the mounds of gargoyle beetles, who darted far from the steps. I was left in paralysis, coming to the realization that the scrows had refueled themselves by consuming the small boy's nutrients and life energy.

The police officers said it was a kidnaping, but they were mistaken. The boy is gone. Many people have been becoming *gone* these days, but nobody seems to put two and two together. Nobody can figure out what gives the scrows perpetual energy. Just watch them from afar, when they think they are alone with someone, and you will see what happens. You will see where they get their nourishment. They don't care who it is either: an infant, a governor, a young bride. They just need to refuel. And the only reason they keep the gargoyle beetles away from us is because the beetles make us sick and the sickness drains our energy.

I know we could just get rid of them, throw them from our homes. But then the gargoyle beetles would come back indoors and plague our comforts once again. Their disease would sicken us, maybe kill us. They would probably still be safer to live with than the scrows, but I'm tired, so tired. I'd rather take my chances with the scrows.

I leave the bathroom and go back to my bedroom, slide beneath the covers. One of them is dancing cloud-like on my pillow and I go to smack it to the floor, but pause. I decide against it. I roll on my back and attempt sleep. The dancing one becomes disturbed with my moisture and dives to the floor, craze-quivering into the hallway.

Above, I see more of them creeping across the ceiling like spiders. They are waiting to be out of fuel so they can drop on me and erase me from the bed. I close my eyes and sigh.

I know I will let them do it to me. I'll just lie here and allow them to soak the life out of me, take all the miseries away. No, I won't fight them. I'm too tired to fight. So tired.

hands to delicate fancyman's hands. That's how she was, always affecting everything around her, molding her environment, making everything smooth and white. And she decorated everything green. Green and white.

In the letter, I tell her about the time we went to the river and watched the flying snakes glide from tree to tree like dragons. Sometimes she would snatch one from its flight and swallow it whole, then smile at me and cuddle with my shoulder. She told me she would never let me leave her, that I belonged to her.

She demanded constant affection, violent affection. Sometimes her sharp teeth would cut my tongue open and she would drink the blood. She never wanted me to leave the bed in the mornings, wanted us to stay there all day, holding me down, her snake-slender body stronger than it appeared, stronger than mine. She couldn't get enough of being loved. If it were up to her, she would have locked us up in a bed-sized tomb for all duration, trapped together with nothing to do but hold each other, make love to one another.

As I write the words into the paper of the letter, it reminds me of her claws cutting into my skin. Sex with her was cat-ferocious, she would slice me, dig deep into my shoulders, my back, hold me so tight around my neck that it would choke an orgasm out of me. Every time she had that look in her demon eyes and mounted me, I had to prepare myself for the possibility of bleeding to death, choking to death.

The lizard-wasps land on my letter and drink some of the ink. Their numbers are enormous these days, too much for me to survive a day without getting stung. The cottage has always been infested by them, a giant nest rules the entire basement, but they used to be very few. I remember how my wife used to snatch them with her arm-like tongue. It was pleasure-burning for me to watch her eat them, watch them slide down her rubber-white neck. She would try to eliminate them all, stand near the basement door and gobble them down until her belly looked pregnant. Then her colorless lips would blow me a kiss.

She always loved the snow, she would run through it naked and the freezing temperature never hurt her, her white body blending with the winter white. Without her green accessories, I would not be able to see her at all: white skin, white eyes, white nails, white teeth, white tongue, white nipples, white, white, white. She belonged with the snow.

I believe she was the child made from winter breeding with a man. It's quite possible. The winter, in its magical ways, could have taken the form of a beautiful woman and seduced some lonely forest ranger into bed with it, crept its icy fingers all about him and made him cum inside of it. Its vagina must have been so cold, so painful for the man . . . unless the man was under a spell, feeling warmth inside of there, feeling safety and content, numb to the ice that surrounded him. Perhaps the man awoke to a frostbitten member, or perhaps he didn't wake up at all, winter's embrace suffocating him into deathsleep. And the winter's belly became fat with a baby girl, delivering her into the world as a cold and lonely freak of nature.

She might as well have been the child of winter. It is as good an explanation as any. Or maybe she was the daughter of a demon, or someone from another world, or maybe she was created in a lab somewhere. I never cared to give much thought to her origin. She was beautiful to me and that's all that mattered.

People always despised her, labeled her an outcast and it upset her so much. She tried to dress herself up like a normal human being, but they always saw right through her, through her green wigs and contacts. They always knew how to hurt her. And she was so fragile, so scared of being hurt. All she wanted was to fit in with them, but they wouldn't have her, couldn't handle her unfamiliarity.

The plastic piles thick outside the window, burying the forest below. I frown on it, always frowning on plastic. I've always preferred the snow. Plastic is everywhere.

The wall begins to call my name, moaning out to me in its in its sensual tone. I want to go to it, but I must finish the letter first.

I mention in the letter that I was not lying when I told her she was more human than anyone I've ever met, more real, more natural. She would never believe me. I'd tell her she was normal and she'd think I was making a joke, more interesting and she'd label it an insult. But she believed me when I said I loved her, because that was something I could prove, something that I expressed regularly. She was such a weak creature without love, so pitiful, so desperate for it.

Sometimes her love for me would become so great that it made me afraid. Sometimes her reasoning would break away from her and she would become like another person, an animal-vicious person, hysterical. Sometimes she would try to cut out my eyes with her razor fingernails to blind me, so that I would be unable to work, so I could not get along without her always by my side. Or she would threaten to cut off my arms and legs to make me completely defenseless to her affection. Or once she tried to physically connect us. She drugged me up with Valium and stitched our mid-section together as if we were conjoined twins. I awoke chill-screaming the next morning, looking at her smiling face, she was not in a bit of pain. It broke her heart when I cut the thread away, separating us. She thought I didn't love her anymore.

Anytime she thought I didn't love her, she would either cry frantic-falling, or went attack-berserk and ripped my face or bit shreds of meat from my limbs. Either way, it wouldn't end until I re-convinced her I could not live without her caress, and she would be so happy that she would keep me within her for several days without letting go. She demanded so much from me.

Upon ending the letter, I tell her that I miss her touch, her voice. I even miss her obsessions and her vicious side, I miss being attacked, I miss the snow. I miss her child-emotions during winter, her hiding camouflaged in the white to jump at me from behind, tackle me into the cold earth to sink deep down into a hole where she could sink her teeth into me. I miss her so much that I cannot handle living without her, that I am coming to join her, coming to finally be with her again.

The room darkens as the plastic fills higher than the window, forcing me into night. The whole valley is full of the plastic, coating the trees and mountains and streams, making them artificial nature. The plastic disgusts me. I wish the snow would fall instead. It never does anymore. The plastic is what killed her. It was the first time she saw the plastic, thought it would be as nice to her as snow. She ran into it without her green accessories after a long night of plastic storming, the white plastic thickly coating the ground.

But it was not like the snow, it was bad for her, hurt her. It was not cold, nor hot, but for some reason she acted as if it was. I heard her screams, all around me, but I could not see where she was ... her naked white body was camouflaged into the plastic. I tried following her voice, but it was echoing in different directions, haunting me, killing me. She called my name, and I called hers, but we were apart. Her body sank into the plastic, eating her, melting her like the snow. I could do nothing, her cries became faint and then gone. I lost her. I searched the valley for days looking for her, knowing she was gone, just trying to find her body to lie with her one last time, but I never found it. After the plastic melted away, I still could not find it. The plastic dissolved her. It was too much for her, ripped her apart, destroyed her. She was too unfamiliar to it, too strange.

The wall can't contain itself anymore, ready to burst. I look up to it, my finished letter under arm, ready for the wall's calling, the plastic numbing the house around me.

A human arm forms from the wallpaper, stretches across the room to me, stretches slowly like white rubber. Then its face and breasts emerge, slithering through the surface, moaning my name.

I take the hand, let its long nails creep across my wrist, cutting deep into the skin, cutting until blood empties onto the letter, burying the words. The writing is ruined, but I do not care. She was reading it over my shoulder as I wrote, pleasing herself with my thoughts.

Another arm stretches out of the wall paper and seizes my free hand, cutting into the wrist to release more blood, rivering down my chest and legs. Then it pulls, the wall takes me over the table towards its surface, strong grasp, pulling with such exhilaration, not willing to give me up.

It takes me to its wallpaper face, presses me against its firm breasts, the wallpaint cool and smooth against my raw skin. The arms wrap around me, wrap tight, and the face on the wall opens its mouth and kisses me, kisses deeply. It opens wide, wider, until it is kissing my entire face, the cold tongue encasing my cheeks my eyes, and then the wall treats my head as if it were another tongue, taking my face inside its mouth, squishing its lips around my neck, moaning in rapture. The arms pick me off the ground and stuff me further into its mouth, sucking all around my rough skin, it becomes like a snake and slowly swallows my body into its insides. I feel the vibration of its vocal chords, moans with pleasure to my taste, as I go down its throat. And once my feet slip through, eaten away from the plastic world, the wall goes flat, back to normal again.

The plastic storm continues outside, growing stronger as the days go by, growing into a bitter-vicious mob. Nobody else understands it isn't a real snow storm outside. They eat whatever is fed to them. They make snowmen out of plastic, go sledding in plastic, have plasticball fights. It never hurts them as long as they make it happy, which is usually all the time. Man smiles at the plastic, and the plastic smiles back.

Drunk and King

Hobble Wat was what they called him, but it wasn't his real name. Just another garble concoction that spewed out of his swirly-stuttering mouth—crusty hole in a tangle-thicket of hairs. He was always up for some dippy fun when good and sloshed, just the type of party king that you'd love to keep around, loud and funny-mean in the back of the bar, criticizing the long-haired waiter for waiting too slowly.

He would say, "Come on, Nancy Boy. Old Hobble Wat here needs another one of them whiskeys. And don't be puttin' any of that ice in it this time. I know you be tryin' to cheat me out of my liquor, ya hear?"

All of the bartenders on the cruise ship knew that getting between Old Hobble Wat and his whiskey was a bad idea. Every once in a while, you'd see him power-bomb someone through a table for spilling his drink. Of course, it was usually Hobble Wat who spilled his own drink in a dizzy sway, but he preferred to blame the people nearby instead. Being an obnoxious barfly was pretty funny to the other drunks. They absolutely loved him. Their barroom hero.

And they especially loved him that time he rolled his jiggle-bouncy belly into one of the cruise ship's life pods and blasted off for a late drunk-driving expedition in the middle of space.

He said, "You know, the good thing about drinkin' and

drivin' in outer space is that there ain't no telephone poles to run in to. Back on Earth, ya can't go one mile without hittin' a couple of them pesky things."

The pod went shutter-droopy through the black, missile in the stars, and the cruise ship behind him became more and more a white dot in the distance. With Hobble Wat pretending to drive the shuttle, not realizing the ship was on automatic, slurring a drinking song, and thinking he was a space pirate—arr-arrs echoing.

These life pods were designed to take its passengers to the closest inhabitable planet, insuring that its occupants would have a safe landing and not have to face the discomfort of getting stranded in space. They're a no-brainer. Even a child could make it to safety. Even a bumble drunk like Hobble Wat.

For his sake, it was a good thing the life pods were created to be so easy. Because he fell asleep after ten minutes of flight, snore-snoring and sleep-mumbling at the top of his lungs.

The cruise staff never figured that somebody would be crazy enough to go for a joy-ride on one of the emergency shuttles, but they never counted on someone like Hobble Wat to be onboard. Drunkards of his breed were unpredictable.

He awoke drool-assaulted, just in time to see a green-gray planet growing larger and larger in his view screen. His voice was a squeak-mumble, "What in Sam Hell is that thing comin' at me real fast? It best not be tryin' to crash into me. I'd hate to have to get out of my spaceship and choke-slam it into some barbed wire." But the planet did not feel threatened by Hobble Wat in the least bit, and continued to grow larger within the view screen until green-gray was all he could see.

He landed on a green section of the planet, full of melted trees and orange poppies. Before Hobble Wat knew where he was, the ship's computer announced, "Welcome to Planet Inatia. Please remain within proximity of the pod until the rescue party arrives. Pod Model XG40 is supplied with enough food and water rations for ten adults to last approximately one month."

"Shut *up!*" Hobble Wat yelled in whiskey rage, ram-booting the com system.

The computer sizzle-chugged, but then continued, "Under federal law, no passenger may interact with the natives of Planet Inatia. Their culture consists of . . ." And Hobble Wat smashed his heel through the panel, breaking it inward, and the computer's voice battered to static. "I said *shut up!* Old Hobble Wat ain't in no mood to be messin' with the likes of you."

Then, leaning back dizzy-groaning, he called to the waiter, "Old Hobble Wat needs another beer over here." Nobody responded. His eyes squeezed close. He said, "I need another beer, I say. Don't make me get out of my chair."

It took several moments before Hobble Wat put himself together enough to realize he was stranded on an alien world. All of the alcohol pleasantries were leaving his system and the bitterness was seeping in. He could feel sharp spears in his stomach sack, and the headache thud-clubbed him into spins.

"If I don't get me some mo' beer soon, I think I'm gonna have to commit harry . . . Krishna."

So he pummel-searched through every compartment he could reach without standing up, expecting to find the liquor cabinet. In a large red drawer, he found the survival kit, brimming full with supplies and medical equipment.

"What kind of cheap emergency kit is this? All of these bandages and ointments, but I see not one can of Pabst Blue Ribbon."

Blunder-digging further, he uncovered a bottle of rubbing alcohol. "Here we go . . ." he said, head spinning at the container.

"I guess this is the *emergency* liquor," as he drank into the acidic fluid. His face went harsh-cringing when he swallowed, two wincing coughs. Then he said, "Now that's got some bite to it," before taking another drink.

After some more buzz-numbing entered his system, warm sigh as the hangover became obsolete, Hobble Wat stepped outside to explore his new found world. His foot went immediately into a puddle of gray ooze-like mud.

"Damn planet," he told the mud. "These was my best pair of combat boots."

It was nighttime, but all four moons illuminated the area lucid bright, ensuring Hobble Wat clear vision—besides the swirl-vision brought on by the alcohol. He didn't bother taking any supplies with him, except for the liquor bottle—only booze was necessary in Hobble Wat's eyes. And he stagger-strolled into the jungle of slime-coated vegetation, slap-slapping at some flying spider-like insects that moved tarantula-slow. Very quick to get lost, he wandered aimlessly away from the life pod, punching the goo-tree limbs that got in his way.

"Too bad I ain't got my gun wit' me. I bet I could get me some good kills in this place."

An overgrown root, thick with fungus and a moss-like substance, caught Hobble Wat's ankle and tumbled him forward. A thud of the head and he groaned out violent. His voice muffled in the green soil, "Damn these trees is gettin' Hobble Wat angry." Lifting his abused face—twig plastered to his forehead and scum in his beard—he noticed the bottle of rubbing alcohol on the ground before him, overturned, emptied.

"Son of a *bitch*," he said, tossing the plastic away. "What is Old Hobble Wat to do for alcohol now? Best be findin' a bar quick."

After an hour of blunder-rummaging through alien terrain, going into hangover mode, Hobble Wat found a dirt road separating the jungle.

"Well, this thing better be leadin' me to a bar or else Hobble Wat's gonna get pissed."

He took to the left—not worried about left being the right direction—waver-rambling up the way, and a burst of song erupted from the blubber man, jolly belly belching, "Oh, we love our ladies. Oh, we love our ladies," trying to scare the hangover away and surface whatever buzz he had left, slap-slapping at the zombie-flying spiders.

A town wasn't too far away, just over a couple hills. It wasn't very large, just a village. Darkness, like a shadow was cast over the entire town. Hobble Wat saw the black houses along the road, rancid strong, melted banana-goo just like the vegetation. The air was slimy-thick as well, and he inhaled lungs full of grease. Muck-pool village coated in sickness.

"Well, let's see if they gots a bar in this dump," he said, rubbing the crust in his beard.

He walked into town, growling at his headache. The whole place shadow-desolate, still, drained. No lights were emanating from the shacks, no people about, no signs of life whatsoever. A town of hiding demons.

The moons reflect-shining in his eyes, he said, "Is there a bartender in the house? Come on now, I'm in need of a bartender." His voice echoed stale. No responses. Then Hobble

Wat realized how silent and dead everything was, terrible stillness. He wondered if the world was out of service, broken. Maybe the town was just an eccentric forest, where the trees grew in the shapes of buildings. Maybe a slimy plague swept through and took living kind with it. Whichever reason, Hobble Wat became worried. But mostly because he knew that bars didn't get fully stocked in ghost towns.

Slap-slapping spider flies—coming in all directions, slow like smoke—Hobble Wat decided for some more investigation. He went into the closest home, warm-soaking on entry. He was not expecting to find alcohol, but he was praying. He could always make some bathtub gin like his daddy taught him, but that required more energy than hangover-Hobble

Wat owned.

The house was slightly lit within, a glow issued from a black-wood box in the corner, just enough to see a mud-sloppy room cluttered with nonsensical items.

"Is anybody in here?" he called. "I be needin' some of yo' whiskey if ya gots any." But the words soaked into the clay walls, quiet.

He saw a shadowed figure within the room, near the green-glowing light. It cold-stared at the invading drunkard, who was whirl-balancing himself in the doorway.

"Sorry 'bout bargin' in here and all, but I be needin' some liquor quick."

The shadowed man said nothing, gleaming forward.

Hobble Wat stepped closer, drool down his chin as he analyzed the silent creature. It was black-skinned, like tar, eyes intensely white, human-shaped but hairless and shiny smooth. Its clothes were ragged-brown, but similar to Earth style. It even had boots like Hobble Wat's.

"What's the matter wit' you? Don't you talk?" Hobble Wat snapped his finger in front of the humanoid's face, but no response, motionless. "You dead or something?"

He touched the glossy skin. It was warm, so the man was not dead, just frozen stiff. Maybe Hobble Wat paralyzed him with fright.

"Well, I don't think I likes you very much," he told the frozen man. "You're not the type of person I be wantin' to drink with."

Jiggle-shifting around, Hobble Wat left the man in paralysis to go to someone more lively. He staggered out of the melty shack. Then strolled the street, looking for a downtown area.

No such luck in this small village. The closest it had to a downtown was a large building like a meeting hall. It was the only illuminated shack—yellow lights fogging out of the window, creeping shadows into the street.

Hobble Wat entered loud, bursting through the door as if to scare whomever stood within. And he saw a whole crowd of humanoids—some tar-skinned, some cocoa, some light gray—but none of them shock-jumped to his entry. They just stood still. Statues.

"What's wrong wit you people?" he said, dancing between them. "Do you all sleep standin' up or something?"

With sparkle amazement, he spotted many natives frozen-sitting around a counter in the back of the room, posing just as people would in an Earth pub, and there was a fat grayish-black man that seemed to be a bartender.

"Is that a bar?" he said, eyes going love-wide as he approached the counter, sitting down on an empty mud-mound stool in front of the gray-black man. "I'll have a double whiskey with no ice," he said, but the bartender did not move. "I'm not gonna ask ya twice. Get me my whiskey."

He eye-wandered the counter flat to see the statue people drinkless. They had bowls of red nuggets, frozen in the act of eating. "What in the Sam Hell? This ain't no bar. This is a restaurant. How am I supposed to get drunk now?"

Roaming behind the bar, Hobble Wat hunted for booze. He only found a small supply of edibles where the liquor would've been. There were red nuggets, green slices, and pots of stringy meat stew. The only liquid he could find was a large barrel of dusty water, off in one corner. "Well, at least they gots food."

He swiped a bowl from a frozen man, picking through the red sticky balls. He took them to a table where a tar woman was sitting. He squeezed up next to her, rubbing her side. Then he pinched her rubber-fleshy behind. "How's it going, girlie?"

She was blank-staring at the table, daze-dreaming. Hobble Wat threw his arm around her slender waist. Nodding his head at her, he bit into a red chunk—chewy and bitter. His face went wrinkle-cowering, and then he cough-coughed a frenzy, gagging at the flavor. Raging voice, "What's wit' these people's taste in food?"

Then he shrugged and ate a few more, choke-hacking during every pungent piece, until his ogre stomach ceased to growl. "Now that's the worst eatin' Old Hobble Wat's had in a long time."

He turned to the dark woman. Surprised, he saw her head was turned, now facing him, disturbed expression at him.

"What's wrong with you?" he said to the dirty-eyeing woman.

Shrugging, he stood up, moved to her other side, and blanketed her with his burly arm again. "Oh, we love our ladies. Oh, we love our . . ."

Then Hobble Wat noticed her move—her head slowly, slowly turning toward him, moving so faintly that Hobble Wat wouldn't have noticed the movement if he wasn't sitting there watching patiently.

"Oh, I get it," he said, realizing what planet he was on.

He stood up, pulling the native woman with him, her chin brushing into his whiskey jungle-beard, and he swung her stiff body around, dancing. "Oh, we love our ladies. Oh, we love our ladies. Especially, when we're drunk."

Hobble Wat remembered hearing something about Inatia earlier in the week. It was one of those planets that the cruise would pass by to discuss, but would never land on to visit. He remembered looking out of a window, rum-buttered and running his fist up and down his forehead, when they mentioned how the Inatians lived at a slower pace than those from Earth. A minute to them was a second to us, and an hour to them was a minute to us.

Hobble Wat couldn't pay attention to the tour announcer very long, wander-dizzy eyes, and missed most of the speech. However, he caught the announcer explain, "There is no common pace of time that every being is bonded to. In some worlds, like Inatia, time moves very slowly compared to time on Earth. In other worlds, time goes by at the speed of light—an entire civilization can birth and die while you sit and drink your morning coffee. But from all of their perspectives, time is moving at a normal speed—one that is just right to get a good, long view of their world before departing to go into another."

Then Hobble Wat realized the power he had over them, so fast compared to all of them. He could do whatever he wanted, and they were too slow to object.

As he gave out a chuckle of glee, dancing the slow-moving tar girl, it hit him—a strong alcohol buzz like a train, jumble-blasting through his forehead. It liquified his nervous system, rolling his head loose from his neck, gurgling with complete satisfaction. Hobble Wat blissful-moaned at the dark woman's slow eyes.

He said, "Now, this is what I call a buzz," as he licked the red sauce from his fingers and beard, stealing another nugget from his bowl.

And when the rescue party arrived for Old Hobble Wat, they couldn't tell him apart from the motionless natives, for he had taken to immobility as well—curled up underneath one of the barroom tables, unconscious in dizzy dreams.

Venus' Triangle

Venus grows sicker and sicker everyday.

Her skin is covering up with insecty wounds, peeling skin-pages that flake to her clothes. She has to shake her black lace dress off between classes to get all the flesh bits off, which are much appreciated by the peppermint ants and goldenhand beetles who reside in the campus dirt. A pattern of circle-scabs runs up the line of her back, painting her similar to a tattooed woman. And sometimes she tongues at a leafy fluid that leaks from her sour openings; she says it tastes like butter rum, but I think she is just trying to be funny.

Humor hasn't escaped Venus, even though everything else has. Most of her family, friendships, future, and so on have withered away. But humor is still intact, lively and strong as ever. She'll even be laughing out loud on her death bed, chuckling to herself while fading into the hint of a whisper.

"Laughter is the only thing that makes the pain go away," Venus always says.

Of course, the pain she is talking about isn't the physical agony, which won't go away until her death. It is the pain of knowing that time is running down, that she won't ever have children, that she won't be able to share her genius with the rest of the world.

Yes, I called her a genius. However, *genius* is not the exact term

I am looking for, because she is not like other intellectuals. Actually, she isn't even considered intelligent to most people, because she can't read or write very well. It is not her fault though, she just has a terrible memory that can hardly store basic knowledge.

The missing memory space is used for something that cannot be found in most human brains. It is a small room full of puzzle-objects created from her subconscious. She says it is just a normal room, like the kind we live in, and she can go in and out of it if she wants to—physically walk inside of her own brain and take anything out that she finds there. I asked if she could take a drummer from her head, and she laughed and said there aren't any people inside. But we could really use a drummer. Ted, the one we have now, hardly ever shows up for practice and ruins most of our concerts. We desperately want him out of the band.

Our band is called *Mushrooms*. Venus plays guitar, and I play bass and sing. Venus used to be the vocalist, but her voice became so soft and raspy that she had to retire the position to me. It's sad to hear her sing on the old recordings and then listen to her now. She had such a spirited voice.

Venus never used to enter my room at night, while I was sleeping. For the first three months of living in this apartment, she didn't even know what my room looked like, always off in her special place, with her special business. Painting, sculpting, creating, toying with puzzle-objects from her brain; she didn't have time to stop and probe around. The only time I would see her was for dinner and to practice.

But recently, she has been sneaking into my room while I am in half-dreams to gentle-kiss my forehead. It's not that it bothers me. I am deeply in love with Venus, even though it is not a sexual love, so the kisses give me a snug warm feeling inside. Nevertheless, it makes me wonder.

Tonight, she glides in the same as always, but does not give a kiss. I lie half awake, expecting her crusty dry lips, but she does not use them. Instead, waking me out of dreamworld to full consciousness, whispering murmur words. She crawls onto my bed with her thick open wound smell. I think she is going to get into bed with me, wrap her sickness body around me, and I will let her do it too. But she doesn't come inside of the covers. Leaning over me, she rubs my shoulders to wake me up, her fragile touch quivering against me. I turn to her face, calm-felt expressions.

In the dimness, she looks as she did three years ago, when I first met her. She dressed like a soldier back then, army jacket and combat boots, with her hair shaved down short. Nobody knew the sickness was in her then, but there were warning signs. Her skin was so pale and delicate, white with hints of yellow. I thought her complection was attractive, but it was the first sign of her disorder. Even then, she looked like death.

"Lucas, get up," she whispers. "I have something to show you."

"What?" My hair goes flat-spiked. "I have class tomorrow."

"Just get up."

She drags me out of bed, too impatient to let me put on clothes, to the living room in my boxers. To the beer-soiled couch, she sits me down and tells me to wait for her to bring it out.

"I pulled it out of my mind," she says.

"Oh no, not another one," I say to myself.

Venus keeps taking these things from her brain-room. Crude artwork usually, made out of a pink fleshy substance, grotesque and haunting. I put some tobacco-dip in my mouth while waiting, wishing I had a cigarette instead. Ever since I moved in with Venus, I had to quit smoking cigarettes. I don't complain though, it is for her sake. Her wither-weak lungs can't handle smoke at all.

As she returns, my eyes go goggling weird. The object

she carries is not of the sticky-meat material as the others. It is more a neon glitter-light molded into a triangle, glowing orange with a buzzing effervescence radiating.

"What is it?" I ask.

"You're not going to believe it, Lucas." Her face crinkle-smiles. "This thing is going to make you rich."

My voice goes soft. "What does it do?"

"What if I told you that this device can put *Mushrooms* on the top of the charts?"

I shrug. Curious. She sits next to me, warmth against my half-naked body, holding it up so I can see closer. I expel my tobacco wad without finishing, into a paper cup, noticing the complexity of her brain-object. It is not just made of light. There seems to be a maze of circuitry, spherical organizations inside of the orange glow. When I touch it, the light fades slightly and I feel its energy seep into my hand.

"I call it the *song writer*," she says. "It helps you write songs by strengthening your creativity and assisting your brain configure thoughts into music."

"I don't get it."

"It seems to have access to the subconscious somehow. If you put it on your head you will hear a song issue from your own psyche. It's like a spaceship, but instead of exploring space it explores the sections of your mind that you don't have access to."

I stand up, pace, turn on the heater. "How can you pull something this complex out of your brain? It's impossible."

"Well, possible or not, here it is. You said the same thing when I told you about the alternate dimension inside of my head. But I proved that true with the objects I've taken out."

I shift back to the couch, plopping down, scraping my back on a couch button. "Yeah, but those objects were sculptures, simple. They weren't technologically-advanced devices like this."

"Well, who understands the human brain? Who knows

what we have hiding away up here?" She taps her skull, just above the large purple birthmark. "I have access to parts of mine that nobody's even dreamed we had. Like I always say, 'thoughts are tangible things.'"

I don't argue further, pointless to even start. When it comes to Venus, *anything* is possible. She is such an outsider that the laws of reality don't apply to her. Actually, I wouldn't be surprised if she was capable of taking *people* out of her brain-room. She would give a new meaning to the term *imaginary friends*.

After my pause, she tells me, "Try it out and see."

I agree. The only way to know for sure is to test it. She has probably tried it out a dozen times already, wrote a dozen songs. Otherwise, she wouldn't have told me about it yet, would've waited to know more about what the device does. I bet she is just experimenting with me, just wants to see if it will work on my subconscious the way it does on hers.

She fits the triangle on me like a headband, orange gleaming through my hair, fizzle-whirs absorbing. Almost immediately, I hear music, startle-jumping me. Popping into my brain like a telepathic message.

"What do you hear?" she asks.

I ignore her, listening carefully.

"Give me some paper," I order.

She takes a binder out of my backpack, and I rabid-grab it from her, stealing a chewed table-pen and writing down the notes. But the song leaves my head too quickly to get it down. I curse myself, flinging the device from my head.

"I missed it," I tell her. "It was *good* too."

"Don't worry, there's probably millions of songs trapped in your brain that are even better." Venus film-smiles, nudging happy with skin flaking onto my chest. "I told you it can make you rich."

Wiping her skin pieces away, "Well, I wouldn't go that far. It might help us write some good songs, but that doesn't mean we'll get rich from it. The bands we look up to aren't even rich."

"You don't understand though. Corporate music usually isn't any good because the bands don't have enough time to write decent songs. They concentrate on writing one or two radio hits, and the rest of their album is filler." She raises the triangle, waving it. "This changes all that. You write such good songs with this in such a short period of time, once you're famous you can produce an entire album of hit-quality songs. Then you'd be looked at as a *legend* rather than a *sellout.*"

"Yeah, but we'd still have to get signed to a major label first. Do you know how difficult that is?"

"Stop your bickering, Lucas. If you're determined and write extraordinary songs, you'll make it eventually."

Now I realize why she is saying "*you'll* make it" opposed to "*we'll* make it." She doesn't have enough time in her to wait for *eventually*. She knows that I will *be* the band in the future, after she becomes a memory. It is up to me to make us famous. Her words slow my thoughts, lowering my dim head. She looks so happy, so excited about the object she's found, but it is so sad at the same time. I try not to show my somber face, shifting to other directions. If she sees me low, it will make her the same, and I promised myself I wouldn't let that happen.

"Try again," she tells me. "I want you to write at least five songs tonight."

She puts the triangle on my head. A speed-bursting song hits me off-guard. I listen for a moment, trying to bring the song to clarity. Venus hands some paper, smiling aflame, but I hesitate to take it. I remember my morning classes and how I need to wake up in five hours.

Taking off the song writer, I explain, "Sorry, I'm too tired for this. I'll work on them after class tomorrow. Okay?"

"Fine." A snooty tone at me.

She is mad because I am not as thrilled with the device as

she expected. Well, I probably would've been if it wasn't the middle of the night. Everyone knows about my crankiness problem. Venus comforts the triangle on her own head, ignoring me. I go to the kitchen for some water. Dehydration is strong from the tobacco-dip. However, all of the cups are dirty—both Venus and I too lazy to clean dishes, even with a dishwasher. So I have to stick my head in the sink—a thick meaty odor surrounding—and drink from the faucet.

Returning, I decide to take a peek at what Venus is working on before going back to bed. The lyrics she has written are *I want to walk through an artificial ocean. I want to swim in a city with a cow and a shark.*

"Wait a minute . . ."

I pick up the sheet and read the rest of the peculiar lyrics. Sneering-Venus rips the device from her head with a *what are you doing?* expression. Then I drop the paper and steal the song writer from her hands. And upon listening, I hear *I want to walk through an artificial ocean. I want . . .*

I take it from my hair and say, "It's the same song."

"What?" Her face puckers, annoyed.

"The song you wrote down. It is the same one I heard before I got up. When I gave it to you, it continued playing. And it is still playing now."

"So," she says. "What are you saying?"

"I'm saying that the same song that came out of my subconscious couldn't have come out of yours as well. The subconscious has nothing to do with it."

"Well, if the songs aren't coming from the subconscious, where are they coming from?"

Pause. Both of us silent. Where *were* the songs coming from? That one song wouldn't have come from both of us, so the subconscious theory can be ruled out. Actually, the songs could've come from Venus' subconscious. The device is a product of her head, so maybe it is a psychic link to songs in the back of her mind.

"What do you think?" I ask her.

She shrugs, upset. The song writer made her so happy, and I had to ruin it for her. Why couldn't I have just pretended? She would've never caught on. Now the device is twice the mystery.

"I'm sorry, Venus." I rub her shoulder, gently to not peel any skin. "It doesn't really matter though. We can still use it to write songs."

"No, we can't," she says. "If the songs don't come from us then they are not ours."

"We don't know for sure. The songs can be from anywhere."

I look away. The room is stale with silence. Venus has her sight to the ground, not noticing my comfort-smile at her. She exhales, faltering halfway through.

"Radio," she says abruptly.

"What?"

"It's a radio," she repeats, shaking her head.

"How can this be a radio?"

"It is. When you move it, the reception changes. I didn't pay attention to why it did that before, but now it's obvious. It's just a radio, a telepathic radio."

"Well, if this is picking up waves from a radio station there would be a DJ on sometime, wouldn't there?" I ask.

She shrugs.

"All we have to do is listen for a DJ."

Sitting her down next to me, her scaly skin crunches against my bare arm, irritating. I cringe at first, but it doesn't take long before I sponge her warmth and forget all about the scabby condition. This whole matter distresses her immensely. The object was supposed to be a special gift to me for being there for her, for being the only person to care. Now she is about to burst teary because her *song writer* is not what she thought it was, and I want to cry as well. She leans against me, gazing to the black ceiling, maybe wandering into her brain-room. I cannot go to sleep and leave her like this. I must stay up to try to put her mind at ease. Laying the triangle on my head another time, I must find out for sure whether it is a radio or not.

Many songs go by without interruption, some are good but some are awful. Venus falls asleep on my chest. Her mouth open to drool on my naked skin, the goopy liquid warming down my belly. After a moment, the saliva turns to freezing and I bolt-wipe it away. Then more dribbles down.

We used to sleep together in high school. When I say sleeping, I don't mean we had sex. We just lay there, pressed together, close as we are now. That's how we spent our weekends back then. We didn't go out drinking with all of our friends and didn't have as much interest in concerts as we had in each other, so we spent our nights in bed together.

We were in love, deeply, but it didn't last. Once Venus became sick and her skin began to peel snake-like, she didn't want to have anything to do with me. She figured it would be harder to leave this world if she was intimate with someone. Not to mention her physical appearance no longer attracted me, hideous wounds and scab-patterns crawling her epidermis. But I still enjoyed her presence. It is probably a hard and tragic thing to get romantically involved with someone whose days are numbered. Just being a close friend is bad enough.

After maybe a dozen songs, I hear a voice from the triangle, jerking me to attention. Yes, it is an announcer, a radio DJ.

"KWXY, the *Firefox*," says the DJ, "music you can sink your teeth into. Up next, we have songs from *Suicide Queen*, *The Toxin*, *Jelly Fish*, and everybody's favorite, *The Sandwich Gang*. There's an all-night party going on, so . . ."

I take it off, gaping mind-wandered at the plastic coffee table. The room is loud with silence—only sounds being Venus' breath and my heartbeat pounding against her face. I'm not going to wake her. Sleep is too good a thing to be interrupted for bad news.

"I'm sorry, Venus," I whisper, brushing her thin hair.

For the rest of the night, I stay with Venus, attempting to fall asleep in my sitting position. But it is difficult. I am uncomfortable and stiff, and I don't want to adjust myself if it means waking her. Also, I can't get the triangle out of my head. Something doesn't make sense about it. There's no station anywhere called *Firefox*, not even a pirate station—and I would know, because I practically run the local underground scene. And every song the device plays is entirely *new* to me.

I put the triangle back on, listening for a song I can recognize or for the DJ to give me clues to where the radio station is. Several hours pass, with the sky going from black to a blue hue, but nothing falls into place. The more I listen, the more foreign the music becomes. Some of the song lyrics are so bizarre and unfamiliar that I can't imagine any of the bands around here singing them. And some of the noises the instruments make are so completely unique that only a thousand-dollar synthesizer could imitate them. One instrument sounds like the result of breeding a saxophone with an electric guitar. I'd like to see what it looks like.

More likely than not, the music is coming from outside of my reality. Like from another planet. Of course, they wouldn't be singing in English if they were aliens. Maybe the device translates the language for me.

Maybe the triangle is picking up airwaves from another dimension. That sounds like a reasonable theory since the device came from the alternate dimension inside of Venus' brain.

Or maybe it is the local radio station in Heaven, or somewhere else on the other side. Maybe it is a time machine that pulls music from the future.

Maybe there is an enormous society living underneath the ground, in total secret, and they have radio stations just as we do.

Any of these theories can be true, but it does not matter. Any way you look at it, these songs are not from *my* world, at least what I know of it. And I'm going to take full advantage of Venus' triangle, whether she likes it or not. She won't be around forever, and that is sad, but I will be around for awhile. I need to think about my future. I need to think about the future of *Mushrooms*. And nobody will believe I am copying the songs, even if I tell everyone about the device. They'll just think it is an extraordinarily creative marketing ploy.

Like other thieves, I will be obtaining riches that I do not deserve. But the difference between me and other thieves is that I cannot possibly get caught.

Multiple Personalities

We garble-saunter down the way, peering through the food shops and hot dog stands, arguing over what to eat. I want Mexican—I'm *dying* for a carnitas tostada—but my assemblage hates to eat meat. They want tofu burgers or peanut stir fry or some other disgusting display of vegetarianism. Just once, I wish I could have a grease-brimming steak smothered in ground sausage and a cup of gravy as beverage. That would be the day, though.

Another assemblage knocks into our shoulder, without apology, leering at us for a moment. Then they continue on, urgent-walking into the nearest office building.

"People are so rude these days," Susan says within our head. "So bitter."

Of course, we are just as bitter as most, especially to each other. I am bitter towards Tucker most of all. He is the part of us that always tries to take over the body, do all the talking, do all the deciding, everything. And then he complains when he doesn't get his way. If he keeps it up I'm going to demand we go to the courts to get him removed. Then he can go plague some other assemblage.

"We're getting bean stew," Tucker argues to us.

"Sorry, Tucker," Mary says. "It's my turn to choose."

"No, it's not." His voice bully-whines. "You had us eat that vomit-soup the other day."

"That was last week, and it was good."

"Yeah, right."

Arne barges in with his hunter's voice. "She's right, Tucker. It's not your turn until tomorrow."

Arne is the oldest of us, probably of forty years by now. Some of the older people got to be put inside of young assemblages. This was to add wisdom to the group. Of course, each of us had a strong characteristic to add. I add the artistic sense.

Before we were merged, I was a painter. Even as a high school student, I won dozens of awards. The teachers made me paint the school a mural over graffiti-walls before I graduated, and it was a giant crab with humans for feet. They called my style, "A chaotic display of surrealism." And everybody thought I would be a famous artist one day.

But that didn't last. After the merging, I could not paint anything. Not only were the hands I had to work with unsteady and backwards, but my assemblage couldn't stop whining at me. Not a single one of them appreciate the creative arts.

"We're going to the salad bar," Mary tells us.

She was added to our assemblage because she is very left-brained. Math came as easy to her as painting came to me. Of course, Susan is good at math too, but she's not a mathematical genius like Mary.

Susan was added for her purity and religious strength. She is the one who prays for us and gives us spiritual guidance.

However, religion is not supposed to be a big thing these days. We say we are Catholic, but it is only for Susan's sake. She was the only one who was religious prior to merging.

We are in Susan's body, by the way. The courts selected hers because it was the healthiest. Both Tucker and I were smokers, so they didn't choose either of us. Mary was too hefty and Arne was too old.

Of all five of us, I'm glad we are in Susan's body. She is

like a piece of art; curve-slender features, brown absorbing eyes, platinum blonde hair streaming down the softness of our back. Being a part of her is the only good that has come out of merging. If we weren't of the same flesh, I would've attempted to be her lover.

We go into a salad bar and let Mary take control of the arms, scooping whatever vegetables she wants onto our plate.

"Don't get blue cheese again," Tucker says.

"I'm getting whatever I want."

"You like ranch. Get ranch."

Mary says nothing, scooping shredded carrots and radishes, macaroni salad, and pasta. As she gets to the end of the counter, she goes straight for the blue cheese. Tucker fluster-moans and resists, pulling our arm away from the bowl of creamy dressing, dribbling goo all over our breasts.

"You prick," Mary yells at him.

She seizes control of the arm and dumps the spoon of chunky dressing on her salad, creating an ooze-lake of white.

"Not too much," Susan says to Mary, weight-warning as usual, wiping the cheese-slime from the shirt. We all feel her fleshy chest-mounds as she cleans, rubbing hard against them. I try to ignore, embarrassed as usual, but Tucker seems thrilled. He goes silent, no longer worried about which dressing we'll eat, curling a smile on our lips.

Mary takes us to a table in a dark corner, as she always does when we eat. I wonder if she was ashamed of her weight before she merged with us, always hiding in the back of restaurants so that nobody would see her make a pig of herself. Now she eats salads instead of pizza and cake, trying to keep healthy so that we don't get as fat as she was.

Tucker cringes as we bite into the blue cheesy lettuce. "How can you like this stuff?"

The eatery is mostly empty. Three bodies are in there, crunching vegetables in the stiff atmosphere. Assemblages usually don't associate with other assemblages, talking amongst themselves instead, leaving this world a dismal-hushing place.

I wish there would've been another way for humans to strive. After the drought of the twenties, our food supply had become so low that it could not support a population of our measure. It was either exterminate the majority of our citizenry or merge multiple beings into a single body. Because the courts chose the latter, most people became miserable. Some think we would have been better off sacrificing our greater half.

Tucker childishly jerks our hand while Mary is trying to eat.

"Don't be so immature," Mary says.

He just chuckles and does it again, causing Mary to yell outside of our head, "Stop!" And all of the other assemblages glare at us.

"Sorry," Arne says to the people in his calm voice.

When we speak through Susan's vocal chords, you can tell who is doing the speaking. We all speak at a different tone or variation. Arne's is a deep version of Susan's voice, mine is a mellow version, Tucker's is a loud and obnoxious version, and so on. I can't imagine how she feels when she hears other people speaking with her voice—-her mouth is moving, her voice is sounding, but somebody else is doing the talking. I would've gone harebrained if they chose my body, twisted.

As Mary brings the fork to our mouth, Tucker tips it and giggles, scattering food onto our lap. She screams with our voice again, "Cut it out, jerk!" But he just does it again on the next bite, cackling. So she rams the fork into our hand, grinding it with all of our strength. A burst of pain ripples through us, jerking us back, and our voice spurts out a shriek.

"What are you doing?" Arne exclaims.

"I'm sick to death of him," she says. "If I have to stay in this body for one more day, I'm going to cut our wrists."

Arne's voice goes heavy-serious, "If you even mention

killing ourself again, I'm taking you to the courts to get you removed."

"Go ahead and take me to the courts," she says. "I want out of this body."

"Yeah," Tucker says, "I want her out of here too."

Fred begins gently, "Look. We need to see a counselor for you two. You know that the courts won't alter assemblages anymore unless the problem is severe. And in that case, they usually terminate the conflicting personality." He falters, trying to get his thoughts in order. "We're going to have to get used to living like this."

We pause. Nobody knew it was going to be so terrible after we merged. Nobody knew there would be so much conflict. When I was a kid, I got sick of my brother because we shared a room, and we always got into fights. Well, sharing a body is a little more extreme.

Susan comes out of the silence. "Why *don't* we cut our wrists?"

We all stare at our plate, frozen, surprised to hear the words come from Susan. I used to contemplate suicide for a long time, non-stop actually, but I decided against it. And Susan was one of the reasons. She is too beautiful to destroy, too pure. She is our temple.

"You're serious, aren't you?" Arne asks.

She shrugs our shoulders. "Why not? What's the point of living now? We've given up our individuality, our souls." She shakes our head. "You people took over my body, took over my life. I just don't care anymore. I can't live like this."

"Aren't you afraid of going to hell?" Fred asks. "Your religion says suicide is a sin."

She shrugs, shakes our head again, but does not respond to his question. Instead she says, "I can't remember the last time I was happy."

"We weren't *meant* to be happy," I say.

They are startled to hear my voice in the back of our head.

I usually don't speak at all, silent, listening to their discussions in our mind. I wonder if they forgot I was here, just now remembering, shocked.

I continue, explaining a theory that has been gushing in my thoughts for the past month, "We sacrificed happiness for the sake of our children's future. The courts knew we would be miserable too, but didn't have a choice. The human race would've been wiped out otherwise."

"That's not what *they* said," Mary interrupts.

"I know, they lied. They said that it would end loneliness, end anti-social behavior, but they knew it wouldn't. The only purpose left for us is to make a child, raise it, then wait to die."

I pause, giving us a bite of salad. And say, "That was the plan they had to decrease our population without literally killing anyone. After we're gone, things will be back to normal. Mankind will live on because *we* gave up our happiness."

They agree with my theory by not speaking, glaring away from the table. The courts said that we would be more happy together, but it was just another illusion over our eyes. I get us up, leave ten dollars for the food, and we go out to the street.It is flurry-cold out here, shivering Susan's frail skin, and our voice stutters a sigh. Everything is stale, empty as usual, so lifeless. The courts thought they had solved the overpopulation problem, but in doing so they've overpopulated our minds.

We decide to take a cab, the only car in the street. We don't speak a word to the assemblage driving, stuttering to ourselves, dazing. And then we go back to our quiet apartment, sitting numb in the dimness, alone with each other.

Between Midnight and Tomorrow

Slipping out of a blear-bickering alleyway, into the streetway for a burst-charge to another drag of darkness, trying to find the quickest and safest passage home. I need to hurry: it is only a few minutes until midnight. *Ticky-tick*, says Clock.

I am usually not out at this time of night, safe in Residence Hall 4608, within my chamber of cozy wool-warmth, hiding high-strung from *them*. But tonight I got held up, held back at the tower pub by the sickly-thin girl with the rickety mop hair, the one I find strangely alluring—crazy ghost girl. I got her number this time, her squirming smile when I asked for it, and I was quite squirming myself.

Her name is Effie—a skip-cute name. And she laughed when I told her mine, throat-laugh like a hum, vibrating funny. Well, I guess *Zane* is of the rare breed, but it is still a suiting title for myself. I figured she wouldn't like me though, knowing how she sneers so at the other men in the tower pub, going *ew-ew* whenever they pass. But I had to try, and I'm glad I did, because on my approach to her, my slick-hipster stride approach, she squeezed her tiny fists with anticipation. Maybe I'm just her kind of guy: freak-funny.

I'm not going to make it home in time, running belligerent, wishing I would've acted sooner with Effie, wishing I gave myself plenty of minutes to get back. You see, I can't get caught in the street after midnight, and I'm at least fifteen minutes away from safety.

I make it to the quad's ravine elevator, leering into the abyss of pseudo-glassed complexes and residence towers—baby-blue and yellow paint splashed across the fronts of the buildings, murals that Mr. Jackson Pollock would agree with. My suburb is on Level One, just below the surface, but it's still *too* far. I realize there's no way I'm going to make it. It's time to think of another plan—got to find someplace to stash myself. Before *they* come.

I sprint-run away from the ravine, toward a dark calmness— an empty section of city. As long as there are no people around, I'll be fine. I just have to hide from the ones meandering past midnight. It shouldn't be difficult either—I am hoping—since most are in bed, safe within their happyland dreams. But I must be careful. No telling what *they* are capable of. *Cold* blood creeping within their bitterness bodies.

Halting at an intersection, all quiet besides the flicker-chattering sign that tells me *Don't Walk* over and over again, reflecting red from the white street on every flash. I should ignore the hypnotic light and do *something*. Find someplace to hide immediately. But there is nowhere that looks safe. I am out in the open—the *worst* place I could possibly be.

Then someone comes, appearing from around a corner in the near distance, drinking from an Irish flask and staggering toward me, slurring a murmur-song while choking on some tobacco harsh. He doesn't know what is about to happen.

"Damn drunks," clubbing my leg with protest. "They're *always* out at this time."

Thirsty-eyed to my watch: eighteen seconds left.

No time. Wandering my sight rapid. If only there was a ladder to one of the business rooftops or maybe an unlocked transporter. An elevator would be perfect, to submerge off of the surface to my home level. But there's nothing. All I can do is run.

Surprised to see my legs working correctly after the number of drinks I slobbered down—trying to consume a little bravery into me, so that I wouldn't be stutter-nervous for Effie. My feet stamp hard within leather boots, pressing against the purple-swirled sidewalk, to the nearest building's corner— shrouded in dark. Then I notice my luck kicking in. Just ahead of me: a *fence*—I didn't see it in the shadows. This business must have a storage yard—a junkyard for the fancy establishment's supplies and refuse. Some relief sweats out of me, dripping.

I've never climbed so sloppy-fast. Up and over, with all my weight on the barbed top, cutting into my belly and arm skin, ripping tiny white flaps as I roll-drop to the other side. Landing thud-like into a pile of metal scraps, tumbling off with plum bruises, my face eats into the artificial soil. I choke-inhale the earthy flavor—wanting to remain there, remain still and silent in the murk, but I cannot stop my curiosity.

My blood trickling. I climb up the metal scraps. Check my watch: it is exactly midnight. Peeking through a crack in the gate, I see the old drunkard frozen stiff with a cigarette in half-raise to his lips—the smoke frozen too, right in midair. Time is no longer moving. *Stopped.*

Then it begins: the drunken man's shadow emerges out of the ground—a claw-hand stretching upward, growing three-dimensional, and a torso-mass follows, twisting into a man-like shape. Then a head appears, mouth opening to shriek. And the drunkard shrinks down and down, blackening as he goes, his rummy expression still frozen as he melts tar-like. He has no clue what is happening, frozen within the moment, as he becomes a puddle of blackness. And the man's shadow forms into a full creature, popping with color. Until the shadow is the man, and the man is the shadow.

A *darkling* is what I call it—a demon with white-pool

eyes shining, albino snake-man with boorish metallic braids, twisted scent surrounding. A narrow face, stretching with hook-like teeth. Its locks of hair lash a slight wind, flexing its risen muscle-knots, howling briefly like a yawn. Then it creeps away spider-weird. Relieving the tension in my head, I lean against the metal's cold and breathe deep, sigh-sighing. *It* is gone, but the *danger* is not completely away. At this time, the night belongs to *them*.

I am now existing between the end of today (which is now yesterday) and the beginning of tomorrow. *Intermission* is what I call it. It lasts for about five hours, but only myself and the darklings experience it. To the rest of living kind, intermission is but a fraction of a second. You're more likely to spot a bullet slipping through the air than witness the happenings within intermission—like seeing your own shadow grow into a snake-creature.

I believe that our shadows are our dark sides, the evil half of our souls that are trapped in a two-dimensional form underneath us. But at night, our dark sides gush out to play wicked-world, without any of us knowing—and I've seen them take all the necessary steps to ensure that nobody ever finds out.

I've tried telling people about them, back when I was in my schooling years, back when I agreed with people when they told me I was crazy. The darklings were absolutely terrifying to me in those days; so intensely that I had to tell other people about them, thinking that they could help me. But how could they do anything even if they believed me? At midnight, they would be frozen and their shadows would become demonic. They were more likely to be part of the problem than part of the solution. No, I've always been alone in this matter, alone with the darklings for five hours everyday.

When I was child-young, I always slept through the time between days. I didn't even realize my situation until I was nine, when I awoke in the middle of the night and saw my mother change into a white-scaled demon and jump-escape out of a window, into the midnight. At that moment, the horror pounding within my heart was more fierce than I've ever had to face. I thought that I was dead at first, thought I died in my sleep and was sent to hell—the emotion within me was something that could *only* be felt within hell. Then I came to the conclusion that my mother actually was a devil or a demon in disguise.

Eventually, I learned otherwise, realizing that time stops at midnight so that everyone can succumb to their dark sides. Myself, however, does not. I have no clue why I am the only one cursed to live through the demonic time period—small samples of damnation. Sometimes I think I've lived an evil past life and this is how I am paying for it.

For thirteen years, I've been avoiding darklings. And it isn't easy, let me tell you. The only way I can be sure to avoid them is to lock myself up in my room, away from everyone's shadows, and keep really quiet. They've never broken into my place, thank God. I guess they don't want to waste their time, since a day to them is only five hours long. However, it was hell when I lived with my parents, spending the endless night hiding underneath my blankets, pretending I didn't exist. And the noises their demon-sides made—screech-growls to each other and scattering in and out of the house—was beyond tolerability. It was what made me the unstable person I am today.

The scrap yard doesn't give me a feeling of *safe*, so I decide to stay here no longer. The pressure will kill me if I remain for the full five hours, just outside of an open intersection where they will most likely gather. My eyes—dry-stiff from the paused air—peep through the fence again. I don't see anything, nor hear anything—besides the clatter-banging noises in the far distance, which *always* plague the night during intermission. The noises sound like the darklings are trying to break the iron lock that holds shut the churlish-veined grating to hell, trying to bring forth the dark side of the world to compromise civilized-kind.

I scale the fence another time, quick and quiet, attempting not to snag anymore skin on the spiked rust-wires, curling my gut inside to avoid them. Noticing an unlit street ahead, while bringing one leg over. All I need is to make it there, dash-dash to safety.

Dropping, my heels clap loud on the pavement, echoing as the clatter-bangings echo. The streets are so stale during intermission, everything empty of sound and movement. Even the phantom-clouds covering the red-yellow moon refuse to move from their place. Before I run, I glance over my shoulder to a flickering of movement coming from my sight's corner.

A crack-jerk lightnings my system as I see the darkling just next to me, the snake-face just a foot away from my breaths. It never left, just hiding and waiting for me to leave the fenced yard, toying. White empty marbles gawking fierce, directly into me. Hook-teeth showing a smile-sneer—their natural expression, fiendish. Once my glance hits its satisfaction and the danger seeps into my glob of a brain, I dart across the white street with heavy stomping boots and drunk wobble-legs, my mind moving faster than my body, like it is about to surge right out its container. Not looking back, don't *ever* look back. I hear darkling wheeze-snarls echoing, frothing. And I pass some old scum-district houses, little building after little building, passing one in each step.

I've never been caught in this situation before, *ever*. They've never seen me until now, which means they know I'm able to exist at the same time as they do. I'm no secret, no *secret*. How am I going to hide from them now?

I turn a corner and then another one, and another. My feet and leg muscles loosen, and my lungs go pounding to burst. Maybe it's useless. Maybe I should give up and die. I throw myself in someone's artificial yard bushes (a common decoration for scum-districts) high enough to cover my body. Needing rest, looking back to see if the darkling is still stalking, eyes red from pressure. But there is nothing behind. Just a droughty street.

It takes a few minutes, but I get out of the dust-gray bushes and put myself back together. This is not good at all. I ran so incoherently that I went in the wrong direction, back toward the tower pub where I came from.

I met Effie at that pub two weeks ago, still not sure what the pub's name is, when she was cough-squawking and hollering at the entertainment screen, watching a local professional wrestling group on the free amateur channel, pulling at her hair-knots in excitement. A guy named Benbo, who often claimed Effie a man or sometimes a penis-wannabe, sitting cool-style at the edge of the bar with eye-shades and a commercial brew, was gargle-laughing at her, as he normally does, calling her a booby for watching pro wrestling, and pissing her off.

"It isn't even a real sport," he said.

I was sitting on the other side of him, pretending to laugh at the crude jokes his happiness brain issued to me. I decided to argue with him for once.

I told Benbo, "Pro wrestling would be boring if it was a real sport. It was *meant* to be an action-packed soap opera, with crazy characters and stories and finishing moves. That's why it's the only sport that survived."

"But where's the competition in that?" he said.

Benbo still likes the old-style of sport. He likes *Competition*. Competitive sports went out of the trend when I was younger, back when creativity took over the public's main interest. Professional athletes went from being multi-millionaires to starving within a two year period, and starving poets and artists became multi-millionaires. The only sport that survived was professional wrestling, because of the creativity involved. It is now considered an art form rather than a sport.

"Competition has nothing to do with it," I told him, grinning.

Sly-guy Benbo just shook his head, thinking *whatever*. My

father always said that masculinity was going to die someday. He dreaded the thought, but he noticed the slight change in male behavior and guessed it would mostly likely happen. Now it seems to be fading, *quickly*, so I think he might be right. People like Benbo are a dying breed.

Because I stood up for professional wrestling, Effie turned to me with her pale ghost-face and smiled BIG, teeth bright against her black lipstick. Then she went back to the wrestling.

The smile stained my thoughts for the past two weeks. One of those hit-and-run images that won't let you go, riding the back of your mind all day long. Benbo doesn't like Effie, thinking she's too dirty and demented and trashy and perverted and bitchy. He might be perfectly right about her, but those are some of the reasons why I like her. She's an ill-crazy outcast like me.

There is no way I can get back home now. I'm going to have to ride out the rest of the five hours in a back alley somewhere, listening to the scrapes and snarls of the darklings all night. It is getting cold too.

I find a hidden safe-spot underneath a nearby transporter bridge, coiled up shaky, boots touching an icy pink stream that does not run, like it is a stripe of puddle. The water has been colored pink just like many rivers on the surface. It is not part of our water supply though, which is underground. It is just another decoration.

"Art can be all around us," said President Terra McKinsey, eight years ago.

White breaths shivering, trying to zone myself out, pretending that I don't exist for a short amount of time. Once the pink water begins running again, I'll know that tomorrow has come. And I'll be safe for another twenty-four hours.

After I get off work, I go to the tower pub to meet Effie as I promised her I would. She's sitting on her stool, hugging her legs, her teeth pressing into a kneecap with a trickle of saliva dropping, when I enter. She smiles BIG at me again, her signature smile, drum-druming on her thighs to a hi-bop bass song on the stereo waves, licking the corner of her mouth while glancing at me.

"Zane-Zane," she calls.

Marching over with my trench coat tapping my leg backs, I say, "Hey, how did you know my name was Zane?"

I am trying to be joke-funny, act comical within her presence as she is within mine, but she makes me so nervous that I have no choice but to tell my jokes badly. I don't even think what I just said can be taken as a joke in the slightest way.

"Zane? Oh, no. You're not Zane, you're Bobby." She plays along.

"Bobby? I'm not Bobby."

"Well, maybe you are Bobby and just don't realize it," she says, winking both of her eyes at me.

"I really doubt that, but there is a slight chance that I am Bobby and have mistaken myself for someone named Zane. What a terrible thing that would be?"

"Yeah," Effie agrees, while chewing her vodka tonic ice. "You would have lived an entire life as Zane when you were supposed to be Bobby. What if there is a Bobby out there who is really supposed to be Zane?"

"I hope not," I say. "I'd hate to get into a fight with this Bobby character, especially over an accidental mix-up of identities."

I motion to the double-nosed bartender to get me my usual, which is the swill beer, so cheap it isn't even labeled.

"You cause trouble," Effie tells me, snickering drunk and scratching at a hole on her fishnet-covered thigh.

Bartender shakes his head and loose neck-skin at me, refusing to give me my beer. "We're out of that piss," he says in a gummy-thick voice.

"Well, give me the next step up from piss beer," I tell him.

Bartender shakes his head and neck-skin again. "Why can't you drink decent beer for a change? All what you drink is cheap urine."

"I'm not drinking for the taste, greebler," I tell him with a smirk.

"Then drink some whiskey," says Bartender, caressing his puffed mustache.

"Whiskey?" I say, almost in agreement, grumbling. I dig into my pocket and pull a crumple of dollar bills out, plopping the giant ball onto the metal-smooth table.

"Haven't you ever heard of a wallet?" Effie says, chuckle-gurgle at me.

"I hate wallets," I respond.

Shuffle through my bills, counting. There seems to be enough for whiskey tonight, happily. It will be the first time in awhile too. I can already taste the acid-burn in my throat, anticipating. So I say, "Okay, time for shots."

Effie responds, "Goody-goody."

We get very into the alcohol, happy buzzes spinning and chime-speaking inside of our intellects. Sobriety wings take off-off. And we get into several conversations concerning professional wrestlers, teeth-shaped action figures, and even pop rocks.

I look at my watch, dizzy-wobble eyes: thirty minutes to midnight.

"I gotta go," I tell her.

Effie bites her bottom lip. "No-no-no. It's still early."

"I've got work tomorrow," I lie, knowing that it is impossible for me to stay.

She puts her hand over mine and smiles her BIG smile at me, shaking her head. I whine in response, "Come on. I *need* to." Resisting her is one of the hardest things I've had to do.

"What you *need* is another drink," she tells me, dumping her shot into my glass—spilling drops onto the sides, sticky.

I compromise, "Ten more minutes."

As I dram down the shot, gag-hacking burn, I hear Effie argue, "You mean *twenty* minutes." I can't help but grin witless. Chuckle-eyed, she says, "Let's get them to play some hop-catch."

"Okay."

Hop-catch is the BIG music style these days. It is kind of like witch-techno, but with some screaming and sometimes bongos. It is mega-bop bassy, Effie loves it. She leaves me at the table and hops to the bar, ordering another gin and tonic and telling Bartender to hit the hop-catch wave, but he doesn't seem to want to.

I'm not going to help her persuade him, thinking that I should leave, thinking about ditching her while her back is turned. But I know it would be rude, and she'd probably never speak to me again.

She takes forever, trying to induce the bartender with her cat-cute facial remarks, persisting. I watch the minutes tick-ticking away, uncomfortably. She needs to hurry, for my sake. I'm just going to leave if I have to, which is something I don't want to do. I'll be labeled *no-fun, no-fun*.

But she returns before it comes to that, mope-frowning and cartoon-sad, sipping at her gin drink. Then she says, "He wouldn't let me play it. He called hop-catch *crap*."

"Oh, poor Effie," I say, trying to be cute but coming off as girly to the male drunkards.

She pouts, "Now I'm sad." And I chuckle at her baby-blue behavior. She is not funny, just trying to impress me with a child-like attitude, which means she likes me, which is all I wanted from her anyway.

"I said I'm *sad*," she roars, upset that I didn't respond to her sadness.

"Oh," I say. "I'm sorry-sorry. Anything I can do to help?"

She raises her arms to me, saying, "Hug me."

Yes, I am positive she is trying to imitate a toddler-cute now. I agree with her conditions though, going *awe-awe*, and cuddling her little goblin body like she actually *is* a toddler. However, her toddler act dies quickly as she grips my cheeks violent, flex-pulling my jaw open and sucking my lower lip into her mouth, rippling it blood-rushed for awhile. She bites down on my tongue, and laughs when I whimper to the pain. Black and green-painted nails crawl up my shirt to dig into my chest, as she slurps whatever juices she can get out of my tasting-hole.

I smirk once she releases my face, embarrassed with how the little girl can take control over me so easily, and she smirks for the same reason. Then she wipes the blood away from my lip with her tonic napkin, saying, "Oops, I bit too hard. I must be a vampire."

"Crap!" I scream, as I see the correct time.

"What's wrong?" Effie asks.

Jumping back, out of my chair, tripping, plastic scatters. It is already *midnight*. Trying to get myself up, get out, before they all become demons. But my legs are caught underneath my collapsed chair and my shock is too strong for me to move cleanly.

Time stops.

I turn my head so that I won't see Effie melt-mutating, don't want to see her demon-side, which will probably be the one to kill me. I am facing some of the bar's drunks by the pool table, glaring at them from my view on the floor as they liquify to shadows, and their shadows grow up-up into the real world. Within the second, the bar is swarming with *them*, stretching out their scaled bodies and wheeze-howling, grumble-jabbering to each other. I think to run, but I am trapped in hesitation.

"Oh, my God," I hear Effie from above. "You're like me."

I snap my vision to her, standing over me with her ghost-face confused, still human, not affected by the time-freeze. And she repeats, "You're like me."

I see the darklings groan-smothering behind her, creep-

crowding up to us, almost surrounding, trapping, with their hissing statements. I glance at the doorway. It is clear for an escape.

"Come on," I cry to Effie, grabbing hold of her wrist and yanking her toward the door.

She rips her arm away from me, pulling herself back to the crowd. I whip around to her, confused, with a *what's the matter?* look on my face.

She shakes her head at my reaction, standing amidst the darklings. "What are you doing?" she asks.

I shiver, gawking at her. She is amongst them, seems to be one of them. Then they pass around her and go toward me. Frozen with scare, I just go deeply into Effie's expression. She must be the queen of the demons, I am guessing. Her dark eyes shimmering oddly. But then I grow even more disconcerted as the darklings shift around, pass me without attacking, ignoring completely. They don't even make eye contact, concentration seeming to be elsewhere, leaving us alone within the soundless, musty-calm bar.

"You don't know who they are, do you?" Effie asks, eyes rolling surprised at me.

I don't know anymore. I must've been wrong about them the whole time. They didn't attack us. They hardly even paid any attention to us. "No, I guess not," I tell her, voice ringing within the empty dry.

She packages her arms around me, mouth open gleeful, grr-ing at me. "You make me happy," she says. "Now I'm not alone anymore."

I alarm-grab her, interrupting, "But what about the demons?"

"Demons?" She laughs crazy-girl at me. "They aren't *demons*."

My eyes bulge out of my head, still shivering. I feel crackpot, shock mixing with the whiskey-buzz, and I can't help but break apart—so frustrated that a tear presses its way to my eye. Then Effie comfort-kisses me, whispering, "Come on. I'll show you."

She takes me outside of the quad, to the natural section of the city, toward Mt. Haloway, which is one of the largest man-made mountains in the country. She doesn't want to explain anything until we arrive, trying to shake some sobriety into herself, smiling excited—a happy little girl.

"There," she says, pointing in the distance as we top a purple and silver-speckled hill, giving us a good view of Mt. Haloway.

I look carefully, noticing the mountain is missing from its usual position. Instead, I see a colossal structure, a spaceship stretching miles across. There are violet and yellow lights brightening the area, emanating from the ship's interior. The darklings are there, claw-climbing in and out of the ship like termites, creating the clattering-banging noises.

"Aliens?" I ask.

Effie nods, dazed by the brilliant lights. "They crashed here almost forty years ago, before we were born. They said they couldn't repair their ship because our world doesn't have the sufficient resources, so they've been trying to build a new one out of what we have."

"They *said*?" My face bewildered. "You mean, you've talked to them?"

"Yeah," she answers. "Back when I was a kid, I saw my father turn into one of them, while I was sitting on his lap. I was paralyzed, even peed my pajamas, but he eventually calmed me down enough to explain his story."

"What are they?" I ask, looking down at the darklings who hustle and plan.

"They are *Waters*. Well, that is what they are called in the English translation. They were named that because their early ancestors came from the water, billions of years ago. They have come a long way since then. You can't even begin to imagine how advanced they are, Zane. They have the technology to merge with another being, hide inside of him, pretend to be his shadow. Do you realize how amazing that is? They have been here this whole time, and nobody has suspected for a second."

"The perfect hiding place," I say, shaking my head.

She goes on, "Their old ship was as large as a golf ball, but could fit almost a million passengers inside. They salvaged what they could from the wreckage, but most of it was destroyed. The most important item was a time-stopping device, which they used for brakes. They programmed it to activate at midnight every night, to freeze the natives' time while building their new ship. It is a primitive ship, so they say, but it will be able to get them back home."

"Why don't they just freeze time until the ship is done? Wouldn't that be easier than working for only five hours at a time?"

"Yeah," she says, "but they don't have a choice. The device can only hold back time for a little while. They said it is like trying to stop a river from running."

"What about us? Why don't we freeze like everybody else?"

"That's what I was wondering," she says. "Even the Waters were confused when they saw me unfrozen. They guess that it's because I was born at exactly midnight—in the split second that everyone freezes. I guess you were born at that time too."

I just nod, astounded by the significance of a split-second.

Then she says, "I think it's funny how they are advanced enough to stop time, but still capable of slipping up." Effie and I are evidence of their imperfection.

We curl up on a fur-grassy knoll, underneath a blue-decorated tree, warming each other from the sharpness, wind frozen in place—Effie roll-pressed around me like a starfish, half-shaking. The violet lights brighten our skin artistic, shifting to pink and blue slightly, and then back to bright purple.

I almost begin to cry, holding the ghost girl firmly. In a crack-voice, I tell her, "I lived my whole life in fear, Effie. It was terrible-terrible. And then they turn out to be friendly this whole time." I feel I've wasted my life being afraid.

"Don't worry about it, greebler," Effie says, patting on my eyebrow. "It's better you found out now than never. You could've lived you're entire life thinking they were demons."

"I guess you're right." I close my eyes, listening to the water-darklings work ant-paced, clattering-banging, trying not to waste any of their time.

Effie says, "You realize that you have an advantage over everyone else in the world, don't you? We both do. We have five hours a day more than everybody else. Our days are longer, even our *lives* are longer. The only reason I graduated from school was because I had an extra five hours a day to study. It makes life so much easier, you'll see. Actually, I kinda *hope* the Waters never fix their ship, and stay forever. It's almost like we have a super power."

I've never thought about that before, I have *free* time. Never in my life have I taken intermission as an advantage, but now I see why it is. I was always so afraid between days that I spent my time writhing paranoid, pretending to be asleep, ignoring reality.

"Yeah, it's great," Effie continues. "I usually spend my time painting or getting extra sleep. Sometimes I even help myself to some free drinks at the pub, but I try not to make it a habit. The Waters would get pissed if they caught me. They are a thoroughly honest people, almost free of sin. They'd never use their technology to cheat anyone."

"If they're so advanced," I begin, "then why do they have to hide from us? How can they feel threatened by a society that is primitive in comparison?"

"They didn't hide from us for their own protection, they hide for our protection. They don't want us to know that there's a universal society out there."

"Why not?" I argue. "I bet they could help our civilization immensely."

"Zane, we have enough Earthly problems to deal with, we couldn't possibly handle any universal ones. Besides, the Waters say we need to evolve further. We need to succumb to our gentle sides, our intellects, and evolve away the wild beasts within us, evolve *war* out of us. To the rest of the universe, war is forsaken, *primitive*. There aren't any wars in space."

She pauses, coughs, strokes my thighs to cook. Then says, "We are on our way though, can't you tell? We evolved enough to stop watching mind-numbing entertainment and adapt a stronger interest in art. Neglecting sports was the most important step we took, because sport brings out our competitive side, our primitive-barbarian side. Art brings out our innovative side."

I nod, not fully happy with the idea, but in complete agreement. The creative create and the savage destroy.

At the end of the five hours, the Waters go back to the positions they started from—completely accurate with locating where they left off. Dolor-blank expressions as they melt back into their shade-beds, giving up all free will to mimic their hosts for another twenty-four hours. And their spaceship melts as well, dissolving into an enormous ink-pool, as the man-made mountain emerges out of the spaceship's shadow.

We continue lounging there, calmly inhaling each other. I realize that I am no longer alone; I've found a partner who can share the five hours of silence with me. Even though she was not suffering as intensely as I was during intermission, Effie still had to face loneliness. Now neither one of us will suffer in any sort of way—because we have each other.

I wonder if we were destined to be together, like somebody made sure that time would freeze just for us, just so we could be together, away from the rest of the world. In a period of silence, entangled sweaty with thick breaths against each other. It sure seems like it to me, as her closeness seeps under my skin, sitting underneath the blue-painted tree. Her sighs are whispering, placid as a ghost, and my head shakes with satisfaction, pure *satisfaction*. And I can't wait until tomorrow.

High-Strung Heroes

I had no idea death would be so crude and painful. It is like getting sucked through a cheese grater as your soul escapes the meat through pores on the skin. And once you put yourself together, looking down on your vacant body, spidery feelings swarm into your life-force—shiver-crawling your limbs and torso, biting your neck in such a way that it curls nervousness in your central sphere, and every single emotion is on complete *edge*.

I have left and returned to my flesh twenty-six times thus far, and I have yet to get used to this uneasiness.

The Heroes, as we are called, gather at Paficito Mountain outside of our bodies, twitching neurotically under the electric-gray atmosphere. On this side, the mountain is a fortress of mirrors and glass, with doors of mercury pools, intense squeals piercing across the blood-red clouds. But on the flesh side, Paficito is a national park, perfect for a Sunday picnic on the bright orange grass.

Dynesta is known for its exotic plants and wildlife. It is one of the most colorful planets of all Earth's settlements. However, it is not the Garden of Eden as the first explorers claimed. It turned out to be the most hostile world of the twelve owned by America.

"What are they like?" asks a squeaky male voice from behind.

I take my glance off of the fortress to see who it is. Roberts. He is one of the oldest of the Heroes in age, yet the absolute youngest in appearance. He is like a forty-year-old teenager—baby face, dimples, lanky arms.

I glance back at the fortress, "Why do you care?"

He stutters, "I just wanted to know about them. I asked Parker and he said that, if anyone, *you* would know."

I stick my finger into the oatmeal dirt. "Have you ever been shot in the stomach before?"

"Huh?" His face crinkles.

"When you get shot in the stomach, your entire body curls up inside—a deep, digging pain. Your nerves go like bruises all the way to your fingertips. And as you're lying on the ground, curled up in a pathetic sort of way, it feels like something is alive inside of you. Something eating at your innards and you can't do anything about it, and your anger and frustration explode at it, as you scream for quick death."

I pause, looking back at his juvenile face.

"That feeling," I tell him. "That feeling of anger and frustration from getting shot in the stomach. That's what they are like."

The old kid sits down to give a good cold stare at the native Dynestan fortress. He trembles harshly, more sensitive to being outside of his body than the others. Maybe because it is his first time out.

"Get ready," I tell him, placing a comfortable arm over his shoulder. "We're going in just a few minutes."

Waiting for battle is about one hundred times longer than the actual battle. An average attack lasts three to four seconds. They are intense, grisly, and tornado-like. Outside of your body, your spirit can move at incalculable speeds. It doesn't have the flesh to slow it down. We are indeed lucky our souls work in this way, too. Without such speed, this war would've been hopeless, because we can only last a maximum of ten minutes outside of our bodies before the flesh dies.

The Heroes are the closest thing the humans of Dynesta have to a military. We are amateurs mostly, volunteers—people who lost their families to the demon-like natives and have nothing to live for besides revenge.

I was in prison for murder before they discovered the creatures. Even though I was innocent, I spent two years molding in the greasy colony's prison, basking in a remorseful and hateful ambience. I was of the first to join the Heroes, most of the prisoners were. They all had stories similar to mine. Stories of unexplained murders, and taking the blame for them. Stories of blood erupting out of one's flesh for no apparent reason at all.

We were unable to prove ourselves innocent until Earth sent our scientists *Lazarus Technology*, as it was nicknamed. It enabled humans to leave the flesh, into the dimension of the dead, and return back unscathed. The first of the scientists to use it was the one who discovered Dynesta's native civilization—a dark, cold society of wire-limbed people. He described them as madmen, crazed beyond comprehension. He said it must be due to their environment—existing within the dimension of the dead must create an unstable behavior. That's when everything came into place. That's when we went to war.

Earth has yet to send us troops. They have been promising for the past year and a half, but not one has showed. There is a rumor that Earth is having its fourth world war and can't afford to sacrifice soldiers to us, but a rumor is just a rumor. Dynesta is usually left in the dark.

So far, the Heroes have conquered many of the fortresses in the dead dimension without military aid, but this one is going to be difficult. This, I believe, is the native capital of Dynesta. I take a few breaths, clearing my mind of thought. Then I turn to jittery Roberts. "Stay behind me, okay?"

He nods, but can't speak.

"Okay, people," I holler to the other fifty Heroes. "Let's go."

We dart across shimmering landscape, bolts of light turning from blue to violet to red, going so fast that we melt to a lightning ooze. As the Heroes start up the hill, five men and I—Roberts included—circle around to the back, slicing through the wind like sails, grinding tension in my temples. We hit the two rear guards, wiry limbs striking at us. But we cut right through them without a fight, my claw-like fingers swiping into one's inside and ripping out its central sphere.

Seeping through the liquid metal door, we screech into the main hall, skimming the corridors—nobody—so we soar up spiral steps to the living quarters, through hundreds of rooms—nothing—then to the roof, skiing across the air—it's clear. I take two men down the side of the fortress wall to the left field, the others left to probe the remainder of the interiors. Dashing straight into battle, into a group of ten natives wiry-charging our way. I rip into two at a time, screaming with my intense emotions, shattering their spheres together, liquid life-force dripping down my hands.

One of my men goes down, his central sphere severed into the claw of the largest spindly creature. And I go at it, revenge as a constant thought, slashing through its neck. Then it plunges its wire arm into my chest, close to my shoulder, explosive pains as he digs for my sphere. Resisting, I slash into its wrist, cutting deep. Then gouge into its chest, rupturing his soul's energy source with a popping of texture.

Jerking my vision around, I see the rest of the natives have been defeated, melting into the electric grass. Roberts stands above them, a snarling devil-beast.

"I didn't know you had *it*," I say, sinking to normal speed.

Anger is what makes a good Hero. The more intense it is, the easier your hands slip through another's jelly-like essence.

"How long has it been?" he asks, calming.

"A little over two seconds."

We hear cheering from over the hill. The rest of the Heroes are laughing and romping to the phenomenal defeat. Roberts and I approach, a spurt of movement and we're there. I look across the battlefield. A dozen native spirit-corpses lie in a pile in the sludgy grass, with the Heroes hopping up and down around them.

Gawking at our fellow amateur soldiers, we notice that not a single man amongst them was overthrown.

I turn to Roberts. "Does this feel right to you?"

Roberts shrugs.

I give it a long thought. Then the idea jerks into my mind. "The town!"

Roberts and I stripe through the field towards human civilization. The dancing Heroes see us race by, stop their bantering, and join us. Gliding across the scenery, piercing sounds as we go against the wind. It takes two minutes to get to the edge of town, wasting so much time to get there, feeling so stupid that we fell into a trap.

Terror stretches across all of our faces as arrive, seeing the wiry demons going like lightning from home to home. We can hardly see the humans when looking from this dimension. They are faint transparencies, attempting to flee. It takes a lot of anger for one to pierce dimensions, a reservoir must be built up from abuse after abuse. Before, they were killing maybe four or five humans a year, because their anger was not strong enough. But now, it's a massacre.

"Let's go," I yell to the Heroes.

But I am stopped by Robert's voice. "*Wait.*"

I turn to him.

"We don't have time. We've got only ten seconds to get back to our bodies."

Our faces go limp, realizing that the old kid is right. Normally, I'm supposed to keep track of time, but my mind must have wandered, overwhelmed by battle.

One man says in a panicky voice, "That's not enough time. We're going to die. Our bodies are going to die."

"Let's go, *now*," a female soldier raspy-screams. "We might make it."

I pause. Silent. Looking away from the men. My head goes down and I squeeze my eyes shut. Then the words ooze out of my mouth, "Forget about it."

When I look, they are gawking at me with estranged faces.

"Forget about our bodies," I tell them. "Even if we have enough time to get back to them, what then? We'd have to wait at least five minutes to rejuvenate our skins before we could leave to fight."

I look to the town's streets. Faint screams like whispers reverberate into my tender ears.

"How many people will be dead by then?" I continue. "A dozen? A thousand?"

The Heroes turn away from me, they aren't listening.

"We are the *Heroes*," I cry. "We have to at least *try* to stop them. Our people are counting on us. Even if it means sacrificing ourselves."

They ignore me, shuffling away.

"Are you that *selfish*?"

Then they dash, lightning-sparks into the distance, heading back to their bodies. I want to scream *cowards* at them, biting my upper lip with frustration, but they are already gone.

My body collapses to the ground, sludge-grass slurping juice off my knees. The so-called Heroes won't make it. Some of them might get back into their bodies on time, but only just before the flesh expires, killing them on the spot.

I can sense a man standing above me, ruffling with the chaos-storming emotions. My face is in the slithering mud, so cold and agitated, alien sensations filling when I touch it. My eyes go up to him. It is Roberts.

"Should we fight?" Roberts asks.

My face buries back into the soil. "Why bother?" I tell him, scratching my eyeballs on the trembling mud. "What good would the two of us do?"

"We might be able to help a little," he responds. "We might as well try."

"Sure," a textured moan pours out of my lungs. "But not yet. I'm not ready to die."

Roberts sits down in the mud beside me. The destruction growing louder behind us, smoke and glassy fires weeping in spirals.

We don't say anything to each other for some time, ignoring the killing sounds and staring at the murky landscape, Roberts rocking back and forth.

"They killed my wife," I eventually tell him.

He pauses rocking, but doesn't look at me.

"She was sitting at our breakfast table, smiling at me with her green lipstick and her pink hat . . . It was a Saturday."

He glances to see my eyes buried past the exotic horizon.

"I know it was a Saturday because that was the only day she would wear that pink hat." My mouth bursts a smile. "She only wore it on Saturdays because she said Saturday was a *pink* day. She had colors for every day of the week, you see. Monday was red, Tuesday was purple, I think Thursday was blue . . . I don't remember what Sunday was. It was probably yellow, no . . ."

I pause with my mouth open, allowing the breeze to hush me.

"From the open window, blue-violet light was resting across her profile and the table plants glistened as they always did. The atmosphere drained me into a comfortable, calm mood. It was such a peaceful day. Saturdays were always such peaceful days back then . . ." My voice cringes, "I thought it was fake when it happened, like a cruel joke of some kind . . ."

I slide my hand from my torso up my face while saying, "Slits appeared on her neck and chest. Thin, hardly visible, but *deep*, ripping upward. Her smile lowered as she glanced down to see herself streaming with blood, and then she jerked up to me in a panicking way. Her eyes were wide and shaking at me, tearing as I stood there frozen. She attempted to scream out to me, but she said nothing. She died with that horrified expression on her face, then fell into her food. I didn't move, blood leaking across the breakfast, dripping onto my lap. But I didn't move.

"*They* killed her." I let my eyes close, but keep talking. "They killed her and I went to jail for it. Being in prison wasn't the bad part, no way. I didn't care about prison. It was the fact that I was blamed for killing my own wife that made me bitter. Bitter towards *them*. All I wanted to do was kill them, the entire time I spent in jail, I wanted to kill them and I didn't even know they existed."

"Revenge," I say. "It's the best tasting thing in this universe."

I don't talk anymore. My mind goes back to the alien soil, smiling at the memory of how many of them I've killed, how many I've made pay for killing my wife.

Roberts lifts himself, waits for a few minutes.

"Do you want to go now?" he asks softly.

I just nod and rise, facing the mass of demons in the distance.

At the end of a brief stretch, we start down the hill. Slowly at first, human-speed, but then we bolt, ignoring the intense wind, heading down the mountain as two streams of light. I give it all I have before they take me down, take me to oblivion. It all happens in a second and a half, killing as many of them as possible, squeezing their murky hearts away with satisfying, so satisfying revenge.

Creatures of the Heavens

"Come on, Hobart, come on."

Trent Thorne was stutter-jerking in his muddy suit, shivering at the gray coldness that blanketed him like bee stings. It had been nearly forty minutes since Hobart left, and he had yet to return.

"Come on, come on," he mumbled over and over, glaring up at the cluttered cloud world where Hobart should have been coming down from, green and pink gases snake-swimming through the atmosphere. Everything looked upside-down on the planet. The ground was a flat plain of dull-brown, barren of most plants and animals. But in the sky, the scenery was vigorous. The clouds were like shelves, bursting with vegetation. Insecty green vines whisper-swinging from their sides at the wrinkled ground.

Hobart said that the clouds were solidified due to the atmosphere's gases mixing with the moisture in the clouds, like putting flour in water. But if his theory was correct, why wouldn't the solidified clouds sink to the ground?

Trent tremble-paced barefoot along the gritty rock surface, near a thorny vine—the same one Hobart had climbed, ascending to the nearest cloud and then out of sight. He refused to let Trent go with him, acting the overprotective older brother as usual. But he was right. There was no way

Trent would've gotten as far. His vertigo would have hit like a truck and he would have been paralyzed up there, stiff-eyed. Still, the creatures among the clouds were far too dangerous for Hobart to face on his own. Trent figured the worst for his older brother.

After ten more waiting minutes, Trent went to the shelter, jerk-shaking as he squeezed under the wood-scrap roof. Usually, he wouldn't stay within the shelter for too long because of his claustrophobia. Hobart made it extra small so that it would trap their body warmth, as his wilderness survival group taught him.

Underneath a blanket, Trent found the last piece of fruit and bit into its sour burst. It was what they lived off of; the fruits of the heavens, as Hobart put it. It fell from the sky, dropping randomly from the trees up there. Everyday, Trent and Hobart gathered the purple-skinned fruit. There was nothing else for them to eat—the red grass and other plants from the soil were poisonous. That was why Hobart had to go up into the cloud-world. The fruit was not raining from the heavens anymore, so he had to get it from the source.

Trent tried not to worry about it. Hobart would be back soon and they would have food again. Then Hobart would fix the communicator so they could call for rescue and go to Ursa—where Trent's children were.

He let the cozy images of his children fill his head, thinking about the last time he saw them. They were climbing into the smuggling compartment of an old friend's space shuttle. He was a nice bushy-bearded man who married a woman on Ursa to become a citizen there. That was the easiest way to become a legal resident. However, Trent's family had no choice but to do it the hard way, the *illegal* way.

Ursa was a planet owned by the Japanese. They built up a pretty good space program, better than NASA, and found the little green planet in another system of the galaxy. Most of the citizens were Japanese, but some were American and

European. They sold land to whomever had the pioneer spirit in them and a large enough wallet/purse to afford it. Otherwise, one had to sneak in, being remarked as an illegal alien by tradition.

At first, not too many people wanted to go to Ursa. But then WWIII broke out and nuclear missiles were hitting close to home. Trent knew that he had to get his family out of there quick, sending his kids as soon as he found a way to smuggle them. But Nikki and he decided to work a little longer to save up money, exchange it at the bank for yen, and then head out a month or two later. Tom, a working friend of Trent's, said he could fly them there. Supposedly, his parents owned land on Ursa.

Trent remembered how little Kera had such a cute frown when she said goodbye, pouting to make her face red. Sammy, on the other hand, was trying to be soldier-strong. He didn't say a single word, shaking his father's hand instead of giving him a hug. His stone-serious expression made Trent laugh, seeing him squeezed within the compartment in his silly little suit and bow tie.

Trent decided to go up after his brother. Thinking, "Maybe he needs help, maybe he sprained his ankle up there." But Trent needed a weapon. Hobart took the only spear—made from a shred of the ship's steel—so Trent was defenseless. He had to make another somehow, out of another piece of the ship's metal.

With that in mind, Trent went into the drab-weeping environment. His hair frail in the slight wind, coughing, twitching. The gravity was strong-tugging, pressing his brain against the bottom of his skull. Glancing at the cloud world, the terrain went miles and miles high. Some parts were like floating forests, others mutating blobs, others spread into webs. Even though the clouds were solid they still rained slightly. Drip-dripping like melting ice, collecting to form the lake—which is where the ship crashed.

It was more like a pond, dreary and silent. Once Trent arrived, his heart went cold-stomped, strong emotions pulsating his eyes to see deeper tones, staring into the calm-hushed liquid. The ghost ship rested in red grass. Only a black staleness emanated from its windows.

They had to make an emergency landing on the planet for some reason—Tom didn't live to tell why. His eyes went panic-wide as they entered the atmosphere, shocked to see the condition of the sky, so chaotic. The hard clouds tore limbs from the shuttle, skinning it, breaking dimples along the shaft. It should have exploded then, before they even reached the ground, but Tom managed to save them somehow—just before his death.

However, seeing the ship wasn't the cause for Trent's dark-clasping emotions. His reaction came from the scatterings around the ship, lying so cold-haunted. They were the bones of Tom and Nikki, who died in the crash.

Hasty-walking to the shuttle, Trent hid his vision from the skeletal pieces. His mind had been zombie-weak ever since that moment after the crash, when he hauled Nikki from the wreckage.

He set her down in green mud, quivering bloody. And she stared at him, a faint smile, hugging the back of his neck with her wrist. Her long auburn hair was blood-glued to the side of her face, river of red down her chest. She didn't say goodbye to him, nor say she loved him, nor say take good care of Kera and Sammy. With a fading voice, glaring at Trent with glossy pupils, she said, "Remember the time we went to the beach and rented that crummy rowboat from the guy with no teeth?" Trent squeezed her palm in reply. "You paid fifty dollars and didn't even care that it was a ripoff, because I said I wanted to go. And then we floated along the coast, embracing calmly until we fell asleep in each other's arms. By the time we awoke, we had drifted out to sea. No land in sight. Then, do you remember what you said?" Trent didn't respond, stroking her bloody hair. "You said, 'let's forget about it, let's let the waves carry us.' And so we did, lying inside of the boat against one another, drunk and warm, rocking back and forth in the water. We could've died out there and it didn't even bother us, because we had each other. You whispered to me softly, saying death would be such a comfortable thing to do together. We would die at the same time, embracing, and when our souls left their bodies they would melt together, into one. Then we'd be with each other forever."

Then she smiled, closed her eyes to hug that memory, and slowly went limp. Hobart took Trent away from her, forcing him to be strong. He built the shelter as quick as he could to lay Trent down, and said he'd figure out what to do in the morning. But that next morning, something came. Some kind of creature (or creatures) scavenged the crash site, ripping apart Tom and Nikki's bodies. They left no meat on their bones, pieces dispersed all around the pond. Neither Hobart nor Trent saw what did it, only witnessing the horrible aftermath.

Inside of the musty black of the shuttle, dust clouds disturbing into the air, Trent fumble-dug through scraps— searching for something sharp for the spear's head, trembling hands through the sheets of wreckage. Nothing. He dropped to his knees, cringing at the thought of going up there unarmed.

He didn't have much of a choice though. Without Hobart, he couldn't fix the communicator, trapped there until death, leaving his children orphans on Ursa. Then Trent sparked an idea as he saw Nikki's purse on a rubble pile. He grabbed it and took it outside—away from the bones—to empty the contents, almost tearing as her scented items fell to red grass. Then Trent replaced the contents with three decent-sized rocks, sighing. "This will have to do."

He went immediately, fast-walking back to the shelter and then to the vine that Hobart had taken. Looking up: the gases streamed violet-dancing, cryptic patterns. He threw the purse of rocks over his shoulder and squeezed a grip around the plant-rope. Then began the climb. He had not climbed a rope since gym class, remembering how his phobia attacked him then. However, this was only fourteen feet, so he did not have much trouble—although he was out of breath.

Trent's palm slapped into the goo-cloud on arrival, hoisting himself over, the rock-purse grinding into his ribs. The cloud tottered slightly, lofty-shaking him, small like a surfboard. Balancing, he kept his eyes up, away from the ground. He was not too high yet, but unsure when a fit would come around. Upward, he saw carpet texture under the above cloud-shelf.

"Time for more," he said.

He jumped, catching the next slimy edge of cloud, slimy like algae between his fingers, but it molded like clay for a good grip. Pull ups—he was never good at them. He could probably do two or three but that was it. As he pulled himself onto the second cloud, he felt that clicking of tendon from flexing his muscles the wrong way, wincing. But he managed to bear onto it.

The cloud was much larger than the first. Twitchy grass and a few large plants grew there. He even saw a lizard-like creature worm-scurry to a bush. However, no sign of Hobart. He was able to get higher on that cloud without actually climbing, because it sloped upward. He crossed, squishy footsteps, the moisture seeping into his boots for a steamy leather odor. Then Trent knew which way his brother went, looking toward the closest vegetated area. It was the largest cloud around, castle-like, holding up an entire forest. However, it required a climb of twenty or thirty feet up a tangle of vines and roots.

"Well, if it's the only way," taking a harsh deep breath.

Nikki was good at climbing. When she first met Trent, she was always up in the trees—a thin squirmy girl covered in gritty scabs. One time, she fell from an oak and broke her face. The scar was prominent enough on her forehead and nose bridge to corrupt her beauty. Of course, it didn't bother Trent at all. She was soul-exquisite even with the scars, scabs, grime-hair, and torn clothes. Other guys didn't notice her eminence until she was older, when she grew out of her tomboyish ways. But it was too late then, because Trent already put a wedding ring on her finger.

Once he got to the other set of vines, he tried putting all of his fears into a little bag in the back of his brain. He tried thinking about Nikki, thinking about how she enjoyed this type of thing. He tried tricking his mind into thinking it was easy and nothing to be afraid of. That was what Nikki always said: "You can trick yourself into believing whatever you want."

Deep breath, held it, let it glide pleasantly. Then he went. Noises were screech-hissing above, like the chains of a playground swing. The good thing about the vines, however, was that there were a lot of them. With vine-crowds clustered around Trent, he felt safer, less out in the open.

He climbed easy, slowly, inching up with his legs wrapped around the thin plant-rope—kept thinking it would snap. Even though he was only a third of the way up, he still felt rather brave. The last time he felt that brave was when Nikki convinced him to go climbing with her. She took him hiking and decided to go the hard way, climb the rocky slopes. Fear was unwavering then, but he did it anyway. Nikki could always overpower his fears.

Halfway up the vine, Trent got the feeling of unsafe. He twirled his ankle around the lower part of the vine, tangling it up to an almost-knot, believing it would catch him if he fell—a safeguard. Trent remembered wishing he had a rope that day with Nikki. He slipped many times, catching himself, bursting heartbeats. But once he got to the top, it was remarkable. The view was terror-intense, and Nikki got him to enjoy it. She wrap-held him close for security, soaking herself into the boundlessness, pleasant-breathing.

"Falling is the way I want to die," she started. "If I ever

get a terminal disease, that's what I'm going to do. Climb the highest cliff I can find and leap off into the freedom. The rushing wind. The setting sweeping to me closer, closer. And I'd reach out of my body to touch the crispness with my spirit. It would be the grand finale of my life."

Trent reached the apex of the vine with a rush of relief. Then he saw the spear sticking out of the cloud, pointing upward. Alone.

"Hobart . . ." he called out, but no answer.

Trent pulled himself over the edge, rolling to a safe distance—the gluey surface glazing his skin sticky. Once he let his eyes circulate, his heart almost dropped from its container. The gigantic cloud-shelf really was like an actual forest. Trees as large as the ones on Earth, smooth with a shiny feel. The pink gases were like mist. The fruit, purple-skinned and ripe, were bulging from bushes all around.

The life was so active and motley-colorful that he could not comprehend it all at once—an ocean reef, but in the sky. There were fish there—oxygen-breathing fish that could swim through the air, furry tails and fin-like wings. A school of jellyfish, purple and blue-speckled, feather-floated down from the trees gently, emitting a drizzling sound.

"Hobart . . ." he called again, reverberating voice.

He could see why Hobart would want to have stayed up there for such a long time. It was magnificent. But Hobart really needed to show himself.

Trent couldn't wait to see little Kera's face. He pictured her excited smile, hopping in her little Ursan dress. He wondered how they were taking to living with a stranger. Of course, the children were in safe hands. The man had known Trent since childhood, he was practically a brother. And then Trent thought about Sammy and his stern face, probably still stubborn-mad because they sent him away. The thought almost made water appear on Trent's face, but something stopped it, something made him forget what he was thinking about.

Movement—from behind some trees. He only saw the movement, not the thing that made it. "Hobart . . ." he called. Then it showed itself, shifting from bushes to face him, hearing his voice. It was a reptile creature, but looked like some kind of shark. The face was larger and flatter, but still like a shark. Its jaws open, dumbfounded, gaping at him with rows of knife-teeth. Then it swam towards him, hauntingly slow. Its wings were similar to those of a manta ray, sweeping across the air with grace.

It didn't attack right away, circling. Trent went stiff, jittering eyes. Once it circled behind him, out in the open air, he ran. Lung-bursting to the trees. But he stopped, tripped to the tongue floor. The rope-vine was still wrapped around his ankle, tangled tight, so strained that he felt his foot deepening numb. The creature took the opportunity, fly-swimming at him.

Trent couldn't get it loose. It dug into his skin with its crawlers, cutting as he struggled to get free. His heart pace burst a whimper from his breath, the flying shark quickening to attack, opening its rows of jaws. And without realizing it, as if it had a mind of its own, Trent's arm swung the purse of rocks across the nose of the flying beast, spurts of saliva coughing from its mouth. The purse exploded open, rocks tumbling over its head and back, landing on the pulpy foam. And it shifted away, going around him.

However, the shark-creature was not like a shark from Earth. When hit in the nose, it did not flee for good. The shark turned around, heading back at him, vicious-swimming as if it was *angry* with him. And Trent was defenseless.

But he spotted the spear near the edge of the platform. Without thought, he scurry-leapt to his feet, hustling to the spear with the shark-creature on his tail. The vine on his ankle trying to trip him up, staggering as he got to the weapon. And he tore it out of the slime, sliding his palm against its slick red shaft—his brother's blood—and whipped around.

The shark charged right into it, full force. The blade entered its mouth and pierced through the top of its rubbery forehead. It dropped immediately to the cloud-sponge. Silence. Trent's breath slow but heavy. And the blood streamed out over the cloud, trickling down the side to create red rain.

Trent hardened a glare at its gurgling body and felt nothing. He avenged the death of his brother and the desecration of his wife's corpse, but it was not triumphant nor satisfying, leaving him with an apathetic face.

Then he glanced back to the forest to see them coming. They looked like a flock of birds—no, a school of fish—fly-swimming from the distance. Dozens of them, perhaps hundreds, from all directions. Just like the sharks from Earth, these creatures could smell a drop of blood from a mile away. And the dead creature at Trent's feet had saturated the scene with a million drops of aromatic blood.

His expression was casual as he cut the vine from his ankle, sighing at the flying sharks in the distance. Then, without second thought, he jumped.

Leaping off into the freedom. The rushing wind. The setting sweeping to him closer, closer. And he reached out of his body, to touch the crispness with his spirit. And before he hit the bottom, he gave a gleaming smile, waiting for Nikki to appear beside him, to hold him close.

Kiss the Sun

I am lazy-lolling in the tickle grass with Sisi smothered into my neck—saccharine purrs and sometimes a twitter. We are watching the animated creatures of the park, hopping and dancing and sliding like snails. There is a bench and a couple of trash cans battling each other, ram-blasting garbage/guts all over the lawn and gobbling them back up again. Also, there is a flying rock, dipping into the happy glass lake for drinking, while cawing at a dirt-blackened mannequin who stumbles drunk in the distance.

Sisi shifts her head from my side, crooked smiling, and presents an innocent stare—the eye-pupils so BIG, balls of black without any white showing. Then she pecks my cheek quickly and goes toward the stars, looking at the great pool of green-violet in space. I join her, easy squeezing, quivering at the dazzle colors, which are enough to inflate you intoxicated. The colors come from the fourth planet, Fizzoro, which was called *Mars* before the 1960's—almost four decades ago.

"I don't care what my father says," I tell Sisi. "I'm glad the Camiri people started their settlement on Fizzoro. They may have caused us some serious problems, but look at what they did to the sky. It's pure beauty."

Sisi sneers crude. "They don't even know what beauty is,

you know. They just put that green haze up there to increase the strength of their sunlight, without even realizing its attractive qualities."

She was right about that. The Camiri don't seem interested in beauty. Nobody is sure why. Actually, nobody is sure about a lot of things that have to do with the Camiri, because they rarely tell us anything about themselves. They're an antisocial race; they'd rather have nothing to do with us, and wish we felt the same way about them. But it's hard for us to accept that, because humans are a curious people. Having been alone in the universe for so long, we are excited to learn more about this civilization, and the fact that they've moved in just next door is too torturous to our human curiosity. Sure we study them from afar—more than a dozen probes swarming in neutral space, which they ignore—but that's not enough.

You would think they moved here to be close to another civilization, but it happened that way only by chance. All that they wanted was Mars—a planet with life-sustaining possibilities—and they didn't even ask us for permission to live there.

"I wonder what the sky looks like on Fizzoro," Sisi says. "All those greens and pinks and blues and purples. I bet its beyond comprehension."

I squeeze her wrist in reply, cold bracelet on my palm. She doesn't turn to me, dazed into the green-violet reflections on the lake. She's off in dreamland now.

Yes, Sisi is a dreamer. You can tell right off by the way she talks to you, always soft and distant. I fell in love with her because of the *dreamer* attitude, but she daydreams so much that it has become a nuisance. She even failed out of school because of her imagination, never paying attention, hunkered within her marvels and gape-eyed to her desk. She does that to me all the time, when I'm trying to speak to her, soaring off into her fairy land and forgetting that I exist, looking with a dumb *huh?* on her face. It gets on my nerves quite a bit now. She's becoming less and less the puzzle-fantasy girl I once saw in her.

But then again, she's so warm-bodied and sensual. Her clothes always so tight to her stomach and she never wears a bra. It is too much for a teenager like myself.

"Why won't you sleep with me?" I ask, restarting an old sizzled argument.

"Toby," her voice goes stutter-annoyed, "you know I'm sick of talking about this."

"I know, I know."

"I told you that I'm not ready yet. I'm going through a difficult period in my life and sex would just make things worse."

"How do you know?" I ask. "You've never even tried it."

"Believe me, I don't need to."

I shake my head *whatever*-like, knowing full well she won't give in. I have been badgering her for the past two weeks now, and *maybe in the future* has been the closest response. It's frustrating to be with a girl as taste-curvy as Sisi and not be able to experience her sexually, especially when she's nuzzle-intimate against your body all the time.

She gazes back to the water, narrowing eyes to an old boot swim-swimming across the mirror, splashy sounds playing with the breeze. Her hair whips onto my face, tasting pineapple into my mouth.

I think I'm going to dump her tomorrow.

I go home to my father, drunk by the fire, lounging half-conscious with his glass of scotch on the chair's arm, whimpering briskly. He is an alcoholic, but not the abusive kind. Not the "watching a spam-scribbling television with a stained wife-beater shirt, a dozen screaming children, a trailer park home, no job, and a pissed off attitude toward the world" kind. No, my dad is more of the lonely breed of alcoholics, enveloped in gloom, pathetical waters in the eye-corners.

I take my father's drink from him and clack-set it on the glass table—we can't afford another whiskey stain on the carpeting. He sway-mumbles at me to give it back, off in Dizzyland, a language of broken words. I put a blanket around him. He sinks into the cozy, into sleep.

Then I putt-putter in the refrigerator for food, finding an old turkey and tater-tot sandwich, taking it to my room with a peanut butter apple and a cottage cheese bowl for company.

In my apartment-style room, I flick on a stutter light, wobbling tense above my desk of cryptic sketches and stacks of movie magazines. To the side, I have a glass cage where I keep my pets, hopping up and about as I enter with food. There is a pet lamp, a pet hat, and a pet telephone receiver. Father brought them home to show me long ago, and I found them so boggle-interesting that I *had* to keep them. But that was back when the animations were rare. Now, they are all over the city, and my three little pets don't seem unique anymore. Father was able to get them because he works for a branch of the FBI that tracks down Semitats—the ones responsible for the animations.

Let me explain:

In order to make the planet of Mars suitable for animals, the Camiri had to bring Semitats along—a minority race on the Camiri's home world. The Semitats are wiry, hairless beings with blue skin and a purple belly. They are biologically equipped with a salivary-like gland underneath their tongues that produces an *animating* fluid. This means that anything the Semitats kiss—or lick or spit on—becomes a living and breathing creature or plant.

First, the Camiri filled the atmosphere of Mars with greenhouse gases, which absorb sunlight and strengthen atmospheric pressure. Because of these gases, they were able to melt the polar caps and create a thick carbon dioxide atmosphere.

Then, the Semitats were sent to the surface of Mars, where they transformed many rocks and minerals to vegetation—oxygen entering through their nose while drooling the fluid out of their mouth. And, in turn, the new vegetation transformed the carbon dioxide-rich atmosphere into an oxygen-rich one. It would've taken hundreds of years without the help of the Semitats, but it only took two and a quarter.

Together, they turned the dead wasteland into an alive astonishing home. Fizzoro, they named it. But the Camiri keep the Semitats horribly, as slaves, utilized only for their animation capabilities.

Twelve years after Fizzoro was born, with forests and oceans blanketing the surface, a handful of Semitats escaped from Camiri clutches. Fleeing to Earth in a small space vessel, and crashing somewhere in Roanoke, Virginia, where they scattered, going separate ways, disappearing.

Most of our knowledge concerning the settlers on Fizzoro was obtained from the runaway Semitats—the ones we located early on, standing out in crowds with their colorful skin. It was difficult to get the information out of them, since they were not very intelligent and hardly capable of picking up on our native language, but we obtained some understanding eventually. None that would help us technologically, but enough to satisfy some curiosity. We discovered that the Camiri are a simple pioneer people and not at all hostile. They breed so quickly that only one planet is not enough for them, needing to establish a new settlement every third decade to prevent overpopulation.

Eventually, the missing Semitats on Earth became a problem. They were compulsively animating every object they came in contact with, some of which should *not* have been animated. For example, an autocar had been brought to life somewhere in New York a while ago. Once it became hungry, the autocar drafted a couple of New Yorkers as its food. It ran them over a few times, coercing them bloody-tender, and then ate them through its hood-mouth.

After a few similar cases, the Semitats became America's most wanted outlaws. That's when we understood why the Camiri had them enslaved, controlled.

There are still fugitive Semitats around today. You can tell because animations are erecting all over, all the time, without anyone witnessing their birth—Semitats must be very cunning individuals. Actually, the animation populace increases every day, so much that it is now commonplace to see furniture marching in a parade, street signs eating rotten hamburger meat, autocars shaking water from their backs, and so on. There have even been protests against killing or abusing animated objects—activists rally at least twice a month.

My father is responsible for finding them, but he hasn't had much luck lately. Maybe it is from all the alcohol. He seems fine-fit for his job in the mornings, even when brutally hungover, but I can't tell for sure. For all I know, he could be spending his workdays at the local bar.

I scoop some cottage cheese and plop it into the animation cage—Dog eats most of it as usual. *Dog* is what I named the living hat. I was trying to be funny with words. I named the phone *Crab* and the lamp *Turtle Sandwich*.

Rolling into my bed, kicking away school books and folded clothes and a plastic hand, I slack-lean on my pillow to chomp-chomp into the peanut butter apple. Before I bite down, mouth open juicy, the phone rings.

"Toby?" Sisi says on the other end.

"Hey, miss me already?" My face goes smug-expressed.

Pause, a wandering of her mind. Then she says, "Okay."

"Okay what?"

"I thought about it on the way home," her voice child-nervous. "I'll do it. I'll sleep with you."

My jaw separates overwhelmed. It was the *last* thing I thought I'd ever hear from her. She seemed so sure of herself before, so positive that she wanted to *wait*. I figured I'd have to marry this one to get anything out of her.

After the silence, "Are you sure?" I even surprise myself with how serious I sound.

"Of course I'm sure." Then she whispers, "Look, I can't talk long. Let's meet tomorrow. Where can we go?"

"Not here, my dad still doesn't like you."

"Well, we can't do it here. Let's meet at the Merry Motel. Say, at noon."

"I have school tomorrow."

"Well, you're going to have to ditch."

"I have a test."

"What would you rather have, the test or me?"

"I'll be there at noon."

She hangs up without saying goodbye, so worried that her mother might pick up the other end. Her mother is not the most trusting of mothers, paranoid of what might happen to her daughter, thinking she's going to get raped or stolen. She usually doesn't let Sisi go out in public, not with anyone, trying to protect her from the outside world. But she is *hurting* her, rather than helping. I'm pretty sure she was glad when Sisi failed out of school, forcing her to stay at home forever.

I *was* going to dump Sisi, but now I won't. No way. If tomorrow goes as planned, I'll probably be with her for months to come. It'll be hell in the long run, but I'll stay with her until I get bored. And she'll never want to leave me, because you know how it is with first loves—you never forget them.

After my food is gone, I coil up fulfilled-smiling. Bed blankets are extra soft when you can't wait until tomorrow. It's like Christmas Eve—no, even better.

Waking up early-early, skip-jumping out of bed and into the shower, stammer-stimulated. The water smokes HOT on my icy skin, cleaning parts that need good cleaning, and using fragranted soap. I should be at school right now, already missed Art and Government. I could've caught four classes before ditching to meet Sisi if I wanted to, but you know how it is when your mind is entangled in sex-thoughts. There was no way I would've been able to concentrate on school work.

The phone rings, but I can't emerge water-soaking to answer it, allowing the machine to do its job. I hear a hint of Sisi's voice from underneath the water-batterings. What is she saying? Listening hard, but she finishes before I catch a word. Panic strikes me. What if she just canceled our date? What if she changed her mind? Girls do change their minds an awful lot, you know. She *better* not have. I'm ditching a test today just to be with her.

Out of the shower, quick, dripping naked onto the tile, hitting the answering machine's button. Sisi's voice: "Toby, I'm already at the room. It's number twelve. Get here in half an hour." She pauses, tired *anxious* breaths. Then, "I love you." End of message.

"Better hurry up," I tell myself.

I throw on some clothes; underwear is most important—putting on my lucky pair, the ones with the glow-in-the-dark smiley face in front—checkered pants, green socks, easy black shirt, one red shoe, one white, some Polo, some deodorant, and I'm ready to go. No need to comb my hair, Sisi likes it ratty and in my face.

Disturb-doddering my way out of the door: "Why aren't you at school?" my father asks from his hangover chair.

Glancing back, his face is slipping off of his head with crude wrinkles, hangover-exhaustion. I continue out the entrance, not about to explain. I don't even care if I get into trouble, just saying, "Can't talk, I'm late." And that is that.

Onto the street, the long walk to Merry Motel—properly named for my purpose—and gawking at the oldest animation in our neighborhood. It is a stoplight that now thinks it is a tree, with plastic-star leaves growing up the shaft, evergreen. As I pass, it switches colors from green to yellow as if to say *hi*. It loves turning green and yellow, but never to red—unless it is angry. All of the neighbors amuse-enjoy the stoplight's presence, treating it as the neighborhood pet, and refusing to chop it down. Instead, they put up a warning sign that tells autocars new to the area that the intersection is *out of order*, but somebody is going to get hurt one of these days.

Downtown, the animations are worse. My feet balance-walking on the living sidewalk, stepping softly so that I don't get it irritated. I pass growl-buildings, sneering mail boxes, all sorts of crawling items that have taken to the insect lifestyle, and so on. A public ashtray snickers at me while I'm impatient-waiting for the *walk* light, insane gurgles. Its tiny legs curled beneath it, dirt-crusty, and its stalk is wire-thin from malnutrition. Animations continue to starve in the streets everyday, and we happily let them die.

I don't make it to the motel on time, almost twenty minutes late, walking across the sun-greased parking lot. I hope she didn't leave in a huff. I *pray*. Wiping slivers of sweat from my neck—not knowing if they are from the sun pestering or from the mounting tension—I arrive at the room marked *twelve*.

Tap-tap the door, but don't wait for an answer. Slowly opening it, not even worried if I have the right room, peeking in to dim lighting—a sheet draped over the lamp. She's perched on the bed, passion-posing for me.

"Shut the door and lock it," she orders, and I do it.

"Come closer." Her voice stirs softly but strong, trying to take control of the situation even though *I* am the experienced one. I obey, her little puppy dog, stepping slowly. Then, "Stop."

We both pause, five feet apart. Her eyes twinkling wet, *scared*. I am also nervous, my heart saying *pity-pity-pity*. And she analyzes me, inhaling the anticipation.

"Do you love me?" she asks.

"Of course I do."

"Before I do this," she begins, "you have to promise not to tell anyone. Not *anyone*."

"I promise."

"You're the only one I've ever trusted enough to do this for. I *know* I can count on you, right?"

I nod, and a smile occurs on the corner of my mouth. I still can't believe she is actually going through with it, actually allowing me to have my way.

"Here we go," she says, sighing, as she throws off her shirt.

Ocean blue breasts bob-sway with the action, rubbing against a BIG violet blotch on her chest that stretches to the stomach, covering most of her torso—azure speckles throughout. I don't even realize it for a second, slowly wondering. It looks like a gargantuan birthmark, or as if a tattoo artist accidentally dumped a vial of his ink on her. Then I figure it out.

"You're Semitat." My voice astounded, squeaky-surprised.

"Only half." She blushes, nervous with what she's revealed to me. "My mother was raped by one."

"But I thought humans and Semitats couldn't mate?"

"If they use their tongues they can. The animating fluid works like sperm. Actually, the Semitat that raped my mother wasn't even male."

I wonder if she can animate. "Can you . . ."

"Yes." She picks up the table clock and presses it to her tongue. The device burr-springs alive right there, developing eyes and a mouth. She lets it loose on the peach-colored carpet and it totter-spins underneath the bed. "I don't have much control over it though, and it's not very powerful in me. I couldn't animate a planet like Mars, I'll tell you that."

I sit down close to her, looking deep, understanding her clearly now—*everything* about her. She almost makes me cry, so perplexed and alone, so *special*. I grade-caress her leg hot, a small blotch of blue on the thigh, and she smiles at me with tears separating from her face. It takes me a moment, but I smile back, sincerely. Then I kiss the purple of her belly.

We don't get into sex right away, stroke-holding each other into comfort. Normally, I would have already been done, a pop-it-quick screw like how I do to the other girls. But not this time, not with *this* one. When the moment comes—purple stomach sticky-warm to mine—we begin. Slowly, passion-pleasing and delicate, as the clock tick-ticks, spinning mad-man on the floor.

"Where the hell were you?" Father asks me as I get home after dark. "Why weren't you in school?"

I don't answer, wriggle-scurrying to my room, shielding my face from him.

"You were with that white-trash whore, weren't you?"

I slam the door, lock it, throw myself on a pile of crinkle-clothes. I can't face him now. He'll want to discuss Sisi and I'm scared I'll slip up, accidentally tell him something without realizing it. What if he already suspects her of being half-Semitat? What if Sisi accidentally dribbled some animation fluid in the house? If just a single drop left her lips, it would've animated whatever it touched. What if Father found an animation here? He wouldn't know for sure, but he would've suspected Sisi. How else can your personal items become living unless a Semitat has paid you a visit? If he asks me about her, I'll choke. I'm not very good at lying, exaggerating maybe, but never lying.

"She's going to bring you down, Toby." I hear ice cubes clink-rumbling in his whiskey glass, his head pressed against the door so that the words reverberate muffle-loud. "She's already got you ditching school. You don't want a girl whose going to ruin your life."

Maybe he doesn't think she's Semitat. Maybe he just hates her.

"I'm sorry, Toby," he says, "but I can't allow you to see her anymore."

What? Who does he think he is? I pull myself to the door and kick it, roar-ramming kick, vibrating his listen-face. Ice cubes marble out of the drink, splatter sound on the floor.

"Screw *you*, dad," I say. "I love her. Do you hear me? I *love* her."

"You're sixteen. You don't even know what love is."

"Hey, *you* don't know. Just go back to your moping and drinking, and stay out of my life."

"I just want what's best for you."

"You wanted what was best for mom too, didn't you?"

"Don't start."

"You thought sending her to the institution would help her, thought it would be *best* for her. A lot of good you did with that one."

Then silence. He won't argue anymore. Footsteps sounding toward the drinking chair, sitting, sigh. I probably shouldn't have said that, but the moment got to me. He's probably the loneliest man I've ever met. I wonder if he really does feel responsible for what happened.

Mother went through a mental breakdown when she was thirty. I don't know what happened exactly, I wasn't with her during the episode and Father wouldn't tell me about it. He had her institutionalized in the county mental ward, where the doctors told him she would fully recover—very soon, they imagined. But little did they know that she was going to cut her wrists on broken toilet-porcelain, and flood her setting with gluey redness. Everyone involved blamed themselves for her death, except for me. I didn't even know what was going on.

For the next week and a half, I spend most of my time with Sisi and very little time at home—and when I do, neither I nor Father journey out of our rooms. I'm missing a lot of classes, but I don't care. This is *love*. I can always go back to school in the future, but this moment is here, *now*. I'm not going to waste a second of it.

We are ease-lounging at the park, as we have been doing every night, snuggle-pressed firmly together. Sisi's not afraid to expose her colored side, open belly button in the air. My heat-massaging hand slithers from the purple to the blue—she likes it when I touch her Semitat skin, but it tickles the human flesh. Staring at the Fizzoro-colored sky, infatuated.

"Are there any others like you?" I ask. "Half-Semitats?"

"I'm positive there are. Halfs have to be the reason why so many animations are being born these days. The last of the original Semitats were captured years ago." She grabs my massaging hand, squeezes gently. "The female that raped my mother had a reason for impregnating her. Semitats are on the edge of extinction now. Their only hope relies on halfs. So I'm positive she impregnated dozens of women just like my mother."

"You're the one responsible for all the animations in town, aren't you?"

"That's right." She grins. "They're all my *babies*." Her voice so excited, like the animations really are her children.

She billow-rolls on top of my gut, warming herself, with her jacket conceal-trapping my sides. Eyes flowing, she smirks at me, as if she wants to do it right here in the park. Then her cheek mashes into my chest.

"I'll probably be weirded-out for the next week," she tells me.

animated body and deranged intellect, I still find Sisi violently attractive, exquisite. I can't picture being with anyone else.

At night, I sneak out of the house while Sisi is in one of her dead-calm sleeps, dozens of paper clips infesting the blanket pile. I need some fresh air, some exercise. The stuffiness is disturbing me into lunacy, and I can't let lunacy happen to me. One of us has to remain sane.

I walk down the main stretch of road, stroll-kicking it slowly. The town is ruined, half-alive and half-overturned, yet nobody seems to do anything about it. Maybe the animations are taking over. Maybe everyone gave up, spiritless, and decided it is too hard to reject them. There are no more Semitats around, so everyone must be boggle-baffled, no clues to why things are getting animated. It would be a lot different if they discovered the existence of half-Semitats. They might actually be able to stop animations from happening. I'm amazed they haven't figured them out yet, probably living next door to one, or have a son that is dating one—like Father.

I wonder what he is up to, wonder if he has changed at all. I haven't spoken to him since the last argument. Maybe I should visit, just for a second, peep through an open window. I'm sure he's drunk, pathetically on his drinking chair, passed out. Nowhere else to walk, I might as well go there. Maybe I'll sneak in and get some of my stuff, hoping Sisi won't animate it, thinking of hiding it up in the closet. I should get some music for the long musty moments, like reggae or gothic. Sisi'll like that.

When I enter Father's house, I see him sleep-sitting in the same old spot by the fire, same old drink in his hand, same old gruff face on his shoulder. He is so sad to look at, a hollowed out man.

Before I get to my room, Father awakes, eyes opening up

red-wide, and he sees me. We stand in gleam at each other. It is as if he is looking into me like a mirror, the old man seeing a young reflection of himself. And I see myself in him, an old hush-fading version of me.

Then a warm expression casts over his face, delighted grimace, thinking I have come back home to stay. He doesn't say anything, just grinning at me, holding back a sob. I'm not sure if it's from the booze or out of love, but for the first time since I was eight, my father hugs me.

"Let's go to the park," I say to Sisi, whose eyes are filming over with yellow, resting on her grouchy bed. "It'll be good for you."

She spittle-drips a sticky line, twirling her sickness hair-snakes, insensate expression. "Is it sunny?" she asks.

"Yeah, but the sun will be down soon."

"We should hurry then," as she rises from her shimmer-blankets, stretching, crusty-dried animation resin on her blue-violet bareness. She creeps coldly about the house-city, finding some snuggle-friends for wearing—making peep-peep noises.

We go to the park and drowse in the vigor, sitting under a tree so calmly and friendly. Sisi is energy-drained from the walk, reclining her lips on my chubby shoulder, buzzing head like a hangover. Sometimes a groan will escape from her weak lungs. Sometimes a shiver.

"I love you, Toby," she says, but I don't respond, grazing my vision across the green lake. I polish her arm instead.

"I want us to go away together." She stares wide-eyed at me, mouth gaping. "We should save up for a boat and sail away, just the two of us, and explore the whole world together."

I nod, glancing down at her skirt as it crawls up my leg.

"Maybe we can find a deserted island somewhere and make it our home. Then no one will ever find us. We can have children and start a new civilization. And everything on the island will be *alive*." Her imagination-eyes sparkle. "I'll kiss the rocks and the trees and the shells that wash up on the beach. I'll kiss our little huts and our boat. We won't need any clothes. We'll be perfectly happy running naked in the sunlight. Then I'll kiss the sun too."

The sun beams bloody and yellow in my face, hazing, encompassing us like a red giant. She simpers at it, warm-cozy against me. I can taste the comfort-emotions that emanate from her, seeping like boiled onion-scent. "I really wish I could kiss the sun," rubbing her face against my arm. "I wish I could just close my eyes, stretch across the sky, and press my lips against the scorching surface to bring it to life."

A white autocar pulls into the nearby parking lot and three suited men jump out, hasty-heading toward us. Sisi doesn't notice them, staring into the sun with yellow water eyes. She says, "It would be our BIG friend in the sky, looking down on us with it's warm, smiling face, watching over us like a mother or God. And no one would ever be lonely again, because company would be just overhead." Then she sigh-smiles, chin leaning on my chest.

Sisi's grin doesn't cease after she sees the men approaching, realizing what they are here for. She just glances at them and pretends not to notice, not wanting to ruin the moment for us. Her eyes glazing wet, holding me. She says, "I love you."

As the men come closer, Sisi recognizes the one on the left. Then her face goes blank in my direction, confused, shocked. She looks from me to the men and back to me, but doesn't say anything, *can't* say anything. I told my father to stay in the car so that Sisi wouldn't see him—so that she wouldn't suspect anything, so that she wouldn't hate me—but he didn't listen. Her eyes go liquidly, shaking her head in disbelief.

I break down as well, slipping drops to my neck. "I love you too," I tell her.

147

She doesn't put up a fight when they take her away, just glancing back at me with her blank expression, red snake-hair whipping like fire at me. Even though her eyes are wet, she does not cry. Too distressed to cry. Scarring me with her image as if to ask me *You'll remember me, won't you?* And my response would've been *I'll always remember you.* Because you never forget your first love.

An Era of Liquid Streets

Drip-dripping was all I could hear. It was what I wanted to hear least, but the silence only amplified it so that even my thoughts went drip-drip-drip.

She was sleeping there so calm as it happened, as if it meant nothing to her, so peaceful.

"Wake up," I said, ruffling her shoulder.

Her face went groggy as I wiped my hand clean of orange muck with one of the soggy towels from the floor. She came stretching and moan-yawning, then turned to go back to sleep. I had to shake her out of it. I needed somebody to talk to.

"What?" she cranky-asked, eyes closed, rubbing a blue foam out of the corners.

"Were you dreaming?" I asked in soft tones.

"You woke me up to ask if I was dreaming."

I shrugged. "No."

"Then why bother me?"

"I get worried when you sleep. I'm afraid you won't wake up again."

She closed her eyes, didn't respond.

The dripping put a dizziness in my guts, a constant dripping from her bed into buckets below. And the smell of it was similar to army fabrics combined with medicines rotten from the sun.

"I'm lonely," I said, ruffling her shoulder again.

Her eyes opened: two cream-yellow balls, the pupils melted away. She turned to me with that look, staring at me. She said I looked all white with a black outline, no detail or color.

"All I want to do is sleep," she told me.

"I need your company."

"I am still with you when I'm unconscious."

"But when you sleep I cannot tell if you are alive or dead."

"Listen to my heart," she told me, pulling my face into her chest, her skin ooze-squishing around me. "I will be alive for as long as it beats."

"Your heart is mechanical," I told her, my words bubbling in her chest skin. "I want to hear your voice."

Her response was the drip-drip-drip of her skin leaking into the pots below.

"We don't have much time together," I cried. "Please, hold me."

She continued dripping.

The buckets and pots swirled with reds and blues and violets, plus green grease floating on top. The disease changed meat and bones into a colorful fluid, something radiant and magical as it slid from the body.

I wrapped her arms around me, the flesh like pudding.

"How are the kids?" she slurpy-asked.

"Just fine," barely audible over the drip-dripping. "They are asleep. So peaceful."

"There's not much of me left, is there? She asked.

I glanced at her soggy lines of leg and paper-flat stomach. "There's lots and lots."

"Then I should sleep."

I crushed my eyes tight. "Yes, you should sleep."

"Kiss me to sleep," she asked, eyeballs melting from her socket and down her cheeks.

I kissed her, let her fluid flow into me, Her tongue entered my mouth and dissolved in my saliva, sinking down my throat.

When she pulled away, she tried saying *I love you*, but gave up after her jaw melted from her face and dribbled down the back of her neck. So she closed her eyes and returned to sleep.

The melting process quickens near the end.

I didn't wish to see her face melting from her head or her breasts sink through her ribs, so I left her. I went into the living room to play the clarinet softly.

The dripping became splashing from the bedroom and I had to play louder, screeching maniacal annoyances into the cardboard living room.

Then I squeezed my eyes tough to cut the circulation, my throat beginning to gag-scrape. And for the 130 pounds of liquid that was now my wife, only a single tear dropped from my eye.

At twilight, I carried buckets of my wife outside for burial. The street was flooded into a river of shiny fluid. The setting sun reflecting blues, reds, greens. The colors swimming around each other, mingling together but not blending into one mud-color.

And when the sun met the horizon, the river of colors made an outline around the lower portions of the sphere, as if the river was a part of the sun—like a chin or perhaps a beard. And as the sun lowered into the emptiness, I realized the river was not a part of the sun, but rather, the sunset.

BONUS
STORIES

GOD ON TELEVISION

CHANNEL ONE

"Last night I had sex with my goldfish. Well, I didn't do it in on purpose. I really didn't want to fornicate with the little slimy creature, but she gave me no choice. In fact, the goldfish didn't even ask for consent, jumping up on top of me and screwing me right against the tile floor. I guess it was a rape or molestation. I didn't know what to do. I just lay there with a squishy look on my face, the cold slimy creature holding me down, slipping her breasts all over me. I didn't know how it could breathe out of the water, gills gasping and fish lips opening for air, as it wiggled on top of me. It was so cold inside, but nice and smooth . . . I guess it wasn't an unpleasurable experience, but ever since then I just can't seem to get reality straight. I can't even look my goldfish in the eyes anymore."

My mind twitters and I forget what I'm talking about. I don't remember where I am. What's going on?

"Mr. Edson?" asks a voice in my ear, making me jump from my seat.

Oh yeah, I must be talking on the phone to somebody.

"Who is this?" I ask the voice.

"It's Saul, from the Porchlight Project," says the voice.

My face continues confused.

"The person you've been speaking to for the past twenty minutes. You keep changing the subject, but I think you were beginning to tell me that you had some food and clothes to donate to our cause."

A clicking noise in my head, "Oh yes, I remember now!"

Long pause.

"Well?" asks the voice.

"Well what?" I ask the voice.

"Do you have anything to donate?"

"Oh yes, I have a ton of that stuff. It's ridiculous. I was just going to throw a bunch of it out before you called."

"Great, just leave the items in a box outside and I'll send someone to pick it up tomorrow morning."

"Oh, nevermind," I tell the voice on the phone.

"Nevermind?"

"Well, I don't want some strange person coming to my door."

"Strange?"

"I thought *you* were going to come," I tell the phone. "I don't trust that other guy with the rusty pickup truck."

"It's a woman in a minivan, not a guy in a pickup truck."

"Even worse. I don't trust those women things."

"Well, you're on my way home. Maybe I can come by after work. Is 5:00 okay?"

An image of my goldfish flashes across my mind. "I can't believe she slicked her fin into my butthole!"

"Okay, make sure the food is in a box outside and ready to go," says the voice in the phone.

I continue, "And it even cried out when I came inside of it. I think we climaxed at the same time . . ."

CHANNEL TWO

There is a knocking sound annoying my ear.

It happens in short bursts twice a minute for five minutes.

It's so annoying.

"Annoying, annoying!" I scream at the knocking sound in the air.

"Mr. Edson," says a voice from behind the front door.

The door opens all by itself and then appears a short young balding man.

"Fucking, who are you?" I shriek at the man.

"Saul," he says. "We spoke on the phone just a couple hours ago. I came to get your donation."

"I didn't donate anything," I tell the short man.

"Per our conversation earlier today it seemed clear to me . . ."

He is cut off by a crackling sound. It comes from the kitchen.

"Oh no, not again," I say to the kitchen.

"What is it?" the man asks.

Saul doesn't look like the most intelligent creature in the world, scratching his head like a not-very-smart thing.

From the kitchen comes my hermit crab, hammering towards us. It is now as large as a person for some reason, squatting by the sliced-sausage table.

"What is that?" Saul asks.

"My pet hermit crab," I say. "I call him Hammerskins."

"It's gigantic," Saul says, stepping back to the door.

The hermit crab shuffles, twisty black and red legs slowly across the carpeting. Its eyes curling, glaring at the young man.

The man screeches, turns away to run as the crab scurries its eyes up and down his body.

"Don't run," I tell him. "Hermit crabs don't like you when you run."

But Saul is already running out of my front door and before I can tell him to stop the hermit crab shuffles after him with violent pinchers.

CHANNEL THREE

Hammerskins returns, dragging the bloody corpse of the donation man as if a bone was retrieved.

The crab gnaws on the man's leg, ripping open the meat like a mutant dog.

"You are not a doggy," I tell Hammerskins, and the crab becomes sad.

The hermit crab claws strips of meat from the man's back and stuffs them underneath its shell. Not eating the flesh, just hiding it up inside of its house.

Gripping the young man between its claws and spidery legs, the crab slowly disassembles the man's head. Crumbles of bone and blood ruin the nice sea-green carpeting. An eyeball pops out into the foyer and Hammerskins jerks a limb at it, snatching it up into its shell. The skull splits open and Hammerskins removes the brain.

It places the thinking organ onto its face as if to eat it, but the nerves dangling from the brain start squirming. Like wiry fingers. They hook into the crab's head, digging inside, molding onto it until the brain is a working organ on the pet hermit crab.

CHANNEL FOUR

"I am terrified of God," says the hermit crab in a shaky tone, the donation man's voice.

I cock my head at the hermit crab.

"I don't want to die," says the hermit crab/donation man.

"I'm far too scared to see God."

"Are you an evil person?" I ask.

"No, I am too scared of what will happen to me if I do anything wrong."

I sit myself on the couch in front of the television.

"I help unfortunate people the best I can," says the hermit crab. "For years, all I wanted to do was help people. If I finish college, I plan to join the Peace Corps. But for now I work with churches and nonprofit organizations. It is important not to be self-centered."

The hermit crab spiders up onto the couch, claws in its lap, sinking into its shell.

"What are you doing?" I ask Hammerskins.

"I want to watch television."

"That television isn't for watching," I tell the hermit crab. "Go watch your own television."

"I'm a hermit crab now," says the hermit crab.

CHANNEL FIVE

I am asleep.

No, I'm awake now.

The goldfish is on top of me again, rubbing my penis with her slime-skin, trying to make me hard.

She is more woman-shaped this time, with arms and legs. They are still fins, but now much more limblike. And the head is more like a woman's head, slender neck. She is still cold and wet, gummy scales, fish eyes, fish lips. But now she has a long white tongue gooing out of her mouth and creeping up my face.

Gills pulsing slowly on her neck as her wet kisses wrinkle my chest skin.

We make love three times.

Lying there, glaring into me with her big fish eyes, slicking back her scales.

"Love you," I tell the goldfish for some reason.

And she kisses me all over with her fishy lips.

CHANNEL SIX

She doesn't go back in her bowl this time.

We are sitting on the couch, watching television with the giant hermit crab who had not left his seat since last night.

"Television is not good," says the hermit crab/donation man.

"I hate television," I tell them. "I never watch it. I don't know why I have it at all."

The fish girl swallows at the air.

"I usually love television," says the hermit crab, "but today TV is very boring. God is on every channel."

I look to the television to see a portly southern-styled man with brown-dyed hair and a white beard.

"Who is that?" I ask.

"God," says the hermit crab. "I already told you."

"What's he doing on TV?" I ask. "What's he saying?"

"I don't know, I put Him on mute."

"TV is even worse on mute," I say. "It captures your attention but you don't know what's going on."

"Well, I don't want to unmute it. I can't handle to hear God's voice."

We continue to stare at the screen. The slimy fish woman rests her head on my shoulder. Clicky fluids flowing inside of her.

Wondering if I can read lips, "What do you think God is saying?"

"He's probably fed up with our disobedience," says the hermit crab. "He probably wants to create hell on Earth."

"Why would he do that?" I ask.

"I think He's ashamed of our imperfections," he replies.

CHANNEL SEVEN

There's nobody outside anymore. Not sure what happened. All the buildings disappeared. My home is still here though. Or perhaps my house has been transported to nature?

"I don't like this," says the hermit crab. "God has more power in nature than in the city. Everything natural comes from God, everything unnatural comes from the devil."

"Is God more dangerous than the devil?" I ask the hermit crab.

He says, "God doesn't like us because we build too much. We make unnatural things and live in unnatural environments. God wanted us to stay like the apes."

The landscape is a forest painting. Sandy purple emotions from behind the deep green trees.

Twilight loneliness.

CHANNEL EIGHT

This morning I am growing grass instead of a beard. It is that itchy kind. The pubic hair of grass.

I glide a razor across my face. It smells like a freshly cut lawn now. The hair on my head is still real hair. And my eyebrows are normal. But all the new stuff is vegetation.

I wonder if God has a beard of grass . . .

I wonder if he has tiny fairylike angels that mow it for him when it gets shaggy.

The fish girl is lying in the tub next to me. Fish face bug-eyed at me. Her lower body is now that of a human's, with a slight pattern of scales that look more like tattoos. But the texture of her skin is a woman's.

CHANNEL NINE

Later today, outside:

I can't go to the super market to buy food because super markets no longer exist.

"We're back in nature," says the hermit crab. "We are hunters and gatherers again."

"Who is the hunter and who is the gatherer?"

"I am a bit of a hunter."

"Crabs are scavengers."

"Fine then, I'll be a gatherer."

"I'm too tired to go hunt or gather food," I say. "There's got to be some kind of civilization. We can order a pizza maybe."

"Let's go inside. Nature makes me nervous."

CHANNEL TEN

There is something in the walls, worms and soil and water, as we enter my home. God is still preaching on television, my goldfish examining her privates as God points at her from the television screen.

I kiss her big fishy lips for some reason and see her eyes are turning more human, turning blue. But they are still big. Cartoon eyes.

"Maybe we can eat your fish?" the crab asks. "She reminds me of something tasty."

"Or maybe we can eat crab?" I ask the hermit crab.

"Let's not eat seafood then."

We decide to open up the walls in the dining room and eat all the worms inside. There are many worms, but we also find a beetle, a bottle of dirty water, and a couple severed fingers.

After a few weeks, we decide to conform to God's world.

"It's hard being an animal," the crab says. "But an animal is much safer in nature than a human."

We sit and watch God speaking and eventually take him off mute.

"This is bad," I tell the fish and crab.

"Yes, but there is nothing to do in nature. It is so boring after living in society for so long. As bad as it sounds God is the most entertaining thing there is."

We listen to God for the afternoon. I do not understand a word that comes out of his mouth.

"His accent is messed up," I say. "Is that the accent of Heaven?"

"No, it's just a southern accent."

"What's he saying?"

"He says that we are free of the devil now, free of social organization, free of corporations, free of technology, free of education, free of the system that has corrupted our world."

"What is wrong with all those things?"

"They are unnatural, I guess. He wants us to be animals."

"Well, at least animals are free to do whatever they want."

"No, he says we aren't allowed to do what we want. We have to watch God on television for an hour a day every day and all day Sunday. And during the rest of our time we spend finding food, making shelter, and raising children. The world will continue this way for the rest of eternity."

"Well, at least we can mate," I say, wrapping my arm around the fish woman.

"Actually, you can't. He says you have to get married to have children. And you must only marry within your race. And impregnation can't be done through sexual intercourse. It must be through artificial insemination."

"But that's not natural!"

"God says what is natural and what isn't."

"God has made everything far less natural than it used to be. Talking crabs and sexy fish women are the most unnatural things I've ever seen."

"Perhaps God is going through a mid-life crisis," says the crab.

"I hate TV," I say.

CHANNEL ELEVEN

The coffee table thinks it is a buffalo now, grazing on the green shag carpeting.

"That's very unnatural," I tell the crab. "It was a table and is alive now."

"Does it have meat inside of it or can an animal be made of wood?"

The table steps closer to my feet to eat some coffee-stained carpet, balancing on the wobbly leg that is missing two screws. I grab the loose leg, a cracking sound and it breaks off. The table rolls over squeak-screaming, blood gushing from the missing limb.

I examine the leg hole. It is wood on the outside, but meat on the inside.

"We'll have steak tonight," I tell the crab and fish.

CHANNEL TWELVE

"There's something wrong about nature that makes me feel small." Sitting with the crab man on the roof at twilight. Eating barbequed table meat. Looking into distances. "I mean sometimes it's overpowering."

"God made it that way on purpose," says the crab. "He wants us to feel small in His world. It's how He proves his power over us. Like a tyrant."

"And now we have to watch him on TV."

CHANNEL THIRTEEN

Back in front of the muted television.

People like to watch television. It is what we are supposed to do. Just how we are supposed to want to live with God when we die.

I think I'm being punished for not liking television. Whenever I used to go outside and somebody would try to talk to me about something they saw on some sitcom or kooky news show and I told them I don't have a TV, they would just drop their mouths like I told them my child just died. And they ask if I'm going to get one but I just shrug and then they become suspicious of me. Like there is something very wrong with me and they should get away very quickly. Tell the authorities on me.

CHANNEL FOURTEEN

Weeks pass and I become a small lawn on the living room floor. The fish woman has mutated into a normal woman, but she can't grow any hair and still has a goldfish smell to her. She doesn't talk and doesn't think to put on any clothes.

The crab man has disappeared. I heard some screaming coming from the other room and I think the fish woman killed and ate him. Or he might have ran away.

She spends must of her time on the couch watching television. Her bare feet scrunching against my back. I can sense she is smiling. Smiling at God. Like there is something about him that makes her happy. I have no idea what it is, but I'm sure he's got her brainwashed. She has forgotten all about me. Doesn't remember her lover who has mutated into grass. I know we can't have sex, but she can at least kiss my blades from time to time.

All that she ever does is watch that evil television.

God, I hate television.

THE
THIRD PLANET
FROM MY SHOULDER

There are nine planets in the sky. Or are there ten sometimes? I have nine tattoos of the heaven-planets going down my right arm in pictures. See. It is slightly somewhat abnormal for a woman to put tattoos on an arm, at least I've never met many women with a lot of arm-tattoos, always getting them around their belly buttons, on their lower backs, around their necks, on the upper portions of their breasts, and so on . . . You know, the feminine areas. I put them all on one arm, nine planets, and people say they are masculine and ugly, but I say they are erotic, more women should put tattoos on their arms . . . Actually, one guy—only one—was deeply attracted to my tattoos, but he still thought I was masculine-gross. He didn't like the way I dyed my tongue black.

My planet tattoos are more than just tattoos to me. They are just like real planets with plants and oceans and people. And it is strange because we, as human beings, are certain that the other heaven-planets do not contain people . . . just the little one we're infesting. But this is not true on my arm. People live on all nine planet tattoos, even the tiny one on my wrist. They are small people, and 2-dimensional, but are quite like you and me. Yes, it sounds peculiar, but I am telling you the truth. Their lives are very human. Complicated and lovely and human. They just have less dimensions than we have. I know all about them because I can telepathically enter their minds and live their lives. I can do this because they are a part of my body.

I look down at my arm now, to the third planet from my shoulder, the blue-green one with the big-big cities. It is funny how all nine planets are occupied by human-like beings, yet not one population is aware of another. The people of 2-dimensional Saturn look to 2-dimensional Mars and see a dead planet. The people of 2-dimensional Mercury look to the 2-dimensional Venus and see an uninhabited rock. And the people of 2-dimensional Earth look round and round and see nothing but empty space. They have all been deceived in some way. Perhaps their governments are responsible. Perhaps their governments don't want the people knowing about planet-neighbors for political reasons, and tell lies. Or perhaps 2-dimensional eyes cannot see the other planets correctly. It doesn't really matter, I guess. 2-dimensional life cannot possibly see the whole picture because they lack a third dimension, one of the most elementary foundations in our reality.

The blue-green planet/tattoo spins very slowly underneath my skin. It ignores the fact that it is a drawing and not a real heaven-planet. Tattoos never know when to conform, do they? They rebel against being stationary just as those who get tattoos rebel against having natural skin.

On the surface of the tattoo, there lives a young man named Moses, named after the planet's first world president who died dozens of centuries ago. This Moses has a studio apartment in the middle of a city called Polloco, which is big-big—comparable to the size of our Germany—and the most artistic people of his world live there. However, these very artistic people are restricted to only two dimensions, living like stick-figure cartoons, and have no idea how limited their artwork is without the third dimension.

Moses is my favorite character within the blue-green tattoo. I love his essence, his tattoos, his antisocial behavior. But he is not a great artist and, therefore, not a great person—at least that is how his co-citizens feel about him. They all know that he hides his art supplies underneath the black line in his room, which is his bed, and hardly ever takes them out to create. He says in a choppy voice, "I will never be the best," and then he goes to sleep or drinks a beer until his eyes befriend blurriness.

Moses goes to a sub shop and buys a long sandwich with circles of meat on it, squares of cheese. Nobody else eats here but him and an obese woman who always rubs her feet while waiting for her sandwiches, yell-talking about the personal lives of famous 2-dimensional people to the crispy owner in the background.

She tells Moses: Heaven is not a place, it is a sandwich.

Then she points to the menu. Experiencing heaven costs only $3.50 for her.

Outside, the raindrops are violently applauding the streets, cleaning beer cans and urine and goo-condoms from the sidewalks. Moses goes across the sloppy traffic to a corner store for some gum, but buys cigarettes. They warm the cold/wet weather out of him. His breaths are so beautiful to me, deep and powerful. I like to enter the minds of people nearby and watch him standing there, his constant slow-passionate expressions, unaware of his intensity.

He goes to his girlfriend's house, but doesn't say much to her. She talks on the phone to her brother while he watches a little girl jumprope outside a window, splashing in rain puddles, singing a song everyone knows. Moses watches and then looks at the floor and then watches again and then looks at a lamp, something smells rancid from the box which is a kitchen, an uneaten pepper pizza or something similar. Then his girlfriend gets off the phone and tells him she has a surprise for him, smile-rushing to the bathroom to put it on. But Moses sneaks away while she cherry-flavors her goopy parts.

He goes into the street and walks the line into a square to protect himself from wetness, sitting and staring at the bouncing rain. Blocky 2-dimensional cars drive by as he watches the water fall, and his eyes go into their path. He imagines darting in front of one of the cars, dropping head first underneath to kill him, send him to heaven which is a skull tattoo on my left breast.

His girlfriend calls to him from across the road, back in her home-clothes, and waves at him to sleep with her.

Moses looks up but doesn't move, stares into her 2-dimensional eyes under wet hair. He doesn't see what he is looking for.

"It's somewhere else," he tells the road.

And he walks away. She calls to him, but he keeps going, darts into the closest bar. He sits down and rubs his 2-dimensional face in his hands, cleaning water from his forehead. It smells like vinegar.

The girlfriend, Siri, follows him into the bar, chasing, sad and confused at his ignore-actions, his rejecting of her. She comes to him, moves softly into his view, sits. He looks her in the eyes again, stares, then drops his head into a fist.

She touches his hand with a *What is wrong, Moses?* expression, but he doesn't respond. Her touch asks him *Don't you love me anymore?* and he can feel it.

"I'm sorry, Siri, I don't anymore."

"Why not?" Siri asks. "Is there someone else?"

Moses nods.

"Who is it?" Siri asks.

"I don't know."

"What do you mean you don't know?"

"I'm not sure who she is, but I'm in love with her. I love the way she looks at me, the way she understands me, the way she makes me feel."

"But who is she? Someone you work with? Someone you saw at a party? Someone you bumped into on the street?"

"No," Moses says, trying to avoid eye-contact. "She is someone inside of me."

Siri cringes her eyebrows.

"A dream-woman, I guess. Someone I cannot reach in the real world, only in my mind."

"A fantasy?" she explodes. "You're in love with a fantasy?"

"She's more than a fantasy, she's *real*, just not of this world."

Siri's 2-dimensional face is slicking wet, tears combined with rainwater. "Do you love me?" Her voice hard-serious, shivering.

"I thought I did. I saw the woman in your eyes before. When we first met. At first, I thought that *you* were my fantasy woman in flesh form, but I realized you weren't once we became close. She was just entering your body to be with me, to touch me. I've only stayed with you because of her."

Siri can't speak, swallowing saliva uncontrollably.

"I'm sorry. I'm in love with her."

And I am in love with him.

I just realize it now, the way I've entered Siri's body so many times to be with him, the way he always looked at me when I was inside her. He *saw* me, he saw right through her skin. Perhaps his feelings started when I first discovered him within my tattoo world. I went into his brain and read his thoughts/dreams. At the same time, I was in *his* thoughts/dreams. I became his *fantasy*.

Before Siri gets a chance to respond, I slide into her body and put her controls on hold. Moses glances up at me and freezes, staring into these eyes, finding me in here. His expressions pause.

"I'm here, Moses," I say to him, Siri's hands still holding onto his. "I love you. I won't leave you."

The boy smiles and kisses my thumb knuckle.

It has stopped raining. We walk quietly back to Siri's 2-dimensional apartment, awkward, scared to break the silence. But we're soft-happy, content. I will stay in Siri's body for as long as possible. Perhaps I can stay forever, even though I'll be within a flat world that is really a tattoo. It is not as complex as our world and our children could never be as beautiful here, but I love him enough to bare with it. I am so alone in our world. All I have are my tattoos.

When we get to Siri's apartment, I press myself into him, saying, "I'm so glad I met you," and stroking his 2-dimensional hair.

But Moses takes my hands away and pushes me back. "Siri, I'm sorry. It's over."

I freeze. Staring at him, confused. He doesn't realize I'm inside her.

"Moses, it's me," I scream. "Your dream girl. The one in your thoughts."

He blunt-stares.

"I have entered your body and Siri's. I am the one you are in love with."

Moses shakes his head at me. "It's not going to work, Siri. I'm not in love with you."

"But it is *me*. I'm controlling Siri's body. Just look into my eyes and you'll find me."

Moses sighs. He glances through Siri's windows at me and shrugs. "I just see you, Siri. She's not in there."

And he begins to walk out of the door, to leave me forever.

"Stop," I cry, running after him, grabbing his shoulders. "I'm not lying. Just look deeper. I'm in here. I *need* you."

But Moses just puts his 2-dimensional finger over my lips to hush me, and brushes Siri's hair out of my eyes. He leans into my cheek and gently kisses.

"Goodbye," he whispers, turning to leave.

My limbs go slack and I slip out of the girl's body to watch Moses go, haunting behind him. He mopes down the wet street, sick with frustration and loneliness. He glances at a 2-dimensional stop sign and then at a 2-dimensional garbage can. His body begins to melt as he walks, spilling into the asphalt, leaking limbs and expressions. And just before I go back to my lonely 3-dimensional world, I see his melted body mix with some rain water, stream through a gutter, descend into a stormdrain.

A HISTORY-LESS PEOPLE

They are too busy to write anything down, not in a book, not on a computer, not on the blank piece of paper in the back of the brain. It's not a defect in these people's memories. They just think it isn't convenient to waste so much present worrying about the past, so they retired history to an old shoe box in the back of a closet somewhere and got on with their lives, living day to day, for only the present and the future.

So a young man walks down the street, forgetting each place that he passes once they are passed. He knows his hair is a charcoal brown and his skin is a light cocoa, and he knows he has shoes on his feet and glasses on his face, but he has no recollection of who he was or where he came from, his parents and siblings just a mystery, his education hidden somewhere deep inside of him. But there is a path under his feet, so he follows it with assurance that he will get somewhere.

A bearded man wearing only red-leather shorts and socks stands in the young man's path, rubbing his plum-sausage face. The young man greet-smiles at him, then glances to a small crew of workers digging a trench along the side of the road, most of which are women.

"Hey, we could use an extra hand here," says the bearded man. "Do you need any money?"

The young man instinctively checks his pockets and discovers two hundred-dollar bills.

"No, " replies the young man, his voice soft and ambivalent. "No, thanks. No. I'm fine."

A young woman with short red hair—one of the shoveling crew, ooze-sweating and sticky with dirt—sees the young man and stops her work.

"Wait for me," the woman calls to him, waving a gloved hand.

The man stops, tightens his red elastic belt, and waits for her.

She sprints to the work-calculating machine—an iron mass of chaos-cluttered buttons with ox-hair growing out of its face and sides. The woman scratches her chin, leaning on a plump thigh, until she finds directions written on the machine's chest. She keeps the young man in her view as she slides a metal wristband—that she has just discovered on her wrist—across the machine's eyes. A dozen bills slip out of a slot, payment for three hours work, as the woman pets the hairy parts of the hulking device.

"I'm hungry," the woman cute-complains, punching her stomach with tiny fists. Then she dashes after the young man with her arms raised like a superhero.

"Hello," she cartoon-says to him.

The man repays the greeting with a stuttered "Hi, hello," as she takes him by the hand to walk him down the sidewalk.

After a few minutes, the young man and the young woman forget all about their meeting and assume that they have been a married couple for years—both of them conveniently wearing wedding rings from a disregarded past.

The young woman smiles and places her cheek on the young man's neck as they stroll.

"It's time we have a baby," says the wife.

"Okay," replies the husband gently. "Okay, let's make a baby."

"I'm hungry," the woman cute-complains, punching her stomach with tiny fists. "Let's get something to eat."

"Let's get something to eat," replies the young man.

They go to the nearest café and sit down. They wait for several minutes. No one is in the dining area. No sounds are coming from the kitchen. They wait an hour and then forget they have waited an hour. And so they wait an hour.

A tiny bald man enters the café complaining about his hunger. He digs in his pockets, but finds only lint and blank paper.

"I will be your waiter," the bald man says, stepping into the kitchen for random work. He does not bother to take their orders. They do not know what they enjoy.

"I have to go to the bathroom," says the young man. "To the bathroom."

And the young woman cocks her head from side to side at him.

He goes to the bathroom and washes his hands, rinsing sweat from the back of his neck. There is a strange person inside the mirror mimicking his movements.

After he comes back, he notices the dining room is deserted besides a pretty young woman sitting all alone in the corner, picking dirt from her short red hair.

He walks across the room, eyeing the woman, wondering if he should talk to her. The young woman looks up at him and smiles, eye-flirting with him. But the young man becomes nervous and turns away, sitting down at the bar.

He sits there for awhile, goggling in space, wondering where the waiter is. The waiter is in the kitchen cooking somebody's food.

When the young man turns around, he sees a young woman hungry-staring at him. She has dirty, yet beautiful short red hair. He smiles and turns away, but the young woman approaches him, rubs his shoulder on arrival.

"Hi," says the young man, "Hello."

173

She repays the greeting and sits in the empty chair next to him. "You are an attractive man," she says in a laugh, agitated by a deep down itch.

"Do you want to have a beer with me?" asks the young man. "A beer?"

"Sure," replies the girl with a chirpy snicker.

They search the room for a bartender, but nobody is behind the bar. Actually, there isn't anyone in the entire café besides a tiny bald man sitting at the end of the bar, smoking a cigarette, waiting to order a drink.

"I don't think we are going to get served," says the young man.

"Want to go somewhere else?" the young woman asks him.

"Sure," replies the man, sneaking his wedding ring from his finger to his pocket.

They go into the street. The sun is down already and colorful people race through the shadows, probably heading someplace very important. The young woman leads him into a random apartment building, finds a vacant apartment for them. As soon as the door closes, she attacks into him, bite-licking and rip-caressing. Neither of them knows if it is love or not, but the performance relieves a mysterious pressure.

Next morning, the young man awakes fresh in his bed. He can't see anything until he finds some glasses on the night stand and puts them on his face. He pulls on a pair of pants and searches for a roommate. His apartment is empty. He must live alone.

There is no money in his pockets and he is awfully hungry.

While leaving his apartment, the young man meets a young woman with short red hair. She is squatting down, staring at something on the ground.

"What's that? What are you looking at?" asks the young man.

"Somebody's written something here on the floor," the young woman says.

The man bends down to see words scribbled in charcoal, staining the carpeting.

They read: WE ARE UNDER THEIR CONTROL.

"What does it mean?" the young man asks her, but she only shrugs.

The young woman glances up at the man and freezes in his eyes. A thin smile curls her face.

"Do you want to get something to eat?" she asks him.

The young man sticks a hand in his pocket. "I don't have any money."

The girl checks her own pockets and smiles, finding two hundred-dollar bills.

"Don't worry," says the young woman. "I'll buy."

And the two walk into the street, holding hands. After several feet, they forget their recent past and assume that they are married.

The young woman smiles and places her cheek on the young man's neck as they stroll.

"It's time we have a baby," says the wife.

"Okay," replies the husband gently. "Okay, let's make a baby."

FILMING THE END OF THE WORLD

From the rotten orange scent rushing into the room, I knew a Gorgonite would be joining me for coffee.

I tried to avoid them by taking my break in the most secluded lounge in the sector—one that only the Rhyians, who were on their sleep break, used. I even dimmed the lights to create an unwelcome feel. But in he came, all three hundred flab-pounds, making squish-squishy noises as he went to the counter for some spicy hot Rhyian curd, which smelled a lot like pastrami.

I leered at him as he slithered into the chair across from me, wheezing breaths through his chest's airholes, and brushing tentacles from his face to give me an elephant-tooth smile.

"What are you looking at, *Gorgonite*?" I hissed at him.

His idiot smile turned into a churning scowl. They didn't appreciate being called *Gorgonites* one bit. It was a popular racial slur that originated out of human mythology, relating to a creature with snake hair called a *gorgon*.

The tentacles on the Gorgonite's narrow skull went fury-squirming, and his eyes curled up as he said, "I didn't realize there was a *human* on the station."

"Why not?" I asked. "It's *our* planet that's about to be destroyed."

The Gorgonite sipped from his mucky drink, nodding. He peered through the window to the reaches of starry space, as if buried in thought.

"I get it," he said. "You're a reporter, aren't you? Come to cover the demolition of Earth." Then he smiled, smug.

That's what I hated about the Gorgonites. They're so smug. They think they're so much better than every other race. When I was in high school, I sat next to a Gorgonite female in Chemistry. If her persistent odor wasn't bad enough, she constantly made sure to remind me her grades were higher than mine, even after I told her I worked nights and didn't have as much time to study as she had.

"Well, it is our original home planet," I told him. "After this week, it will be gone forever. Because of *your* kind."

"Would you prefer we left Earth alone?" he asked.

"Of course."

The Gorgonite shook his tentacled head, fanning putrid body odor at me. "It's just like a human to put sentiment over the safety of the galaxy."

Slamming my fist, "There's no proof that the A Bugs are going to spread."

"You must be joking." His voice was drivel-spitting. "They can leave Earth at any time. All they need to do is sweep across the void to Mars. Then *another* planet will have to be evacuated." He clenched a fist. "And I have family in the colonies."

"It's idiotic to think A Bugs will travel through space."

"How do you think they got to Earth?"

"They were riding the comet," I told him. "Every planet it crossed became infected."

"Yeah, but the comet didn't crash into Earth. The A Bugs had to travel through space to get there. And the distance from the comet to Earth was only two-thirds the distance from Earth to Mars. It's definitely possible." He smug-smiled again. "You humans don't care about the A Bugs spreading because there aren't any humans living on Mars anymore."

"Just because your people have settlements on Mars and Europa, doesn't mean you own the whole solar system."

"Well, guess what?" he said, flaming eyes at me. "We *do* own the solar system. We own Mars and we're going to make it utopian, something your kind was too lazy to do. And at the end of the week, we're going to blow your ancestors' worthless dead planet into tiny bits."

I didn't respond, staring into my half-cup of cold coffee. The Gorgonite's rage surprised me. They were supposed to be adverse to anger, leaning more to their peaceful side. I guess that is just another stereotype.

"Look." His voice went calm. "Every time I meet up with one of you, it's always the same argument. You people have a bitterness inside of you that I cannot begin to comprehend." He paused to drink. "I suggest we ignore each other for the rest of the break."

I nodded, then glanced down to the newsscreen I had been scanning. However, my mind was so wander-rushing that I could not read a word. It was the first real confrontation I had with a Gorgonite all week. Before then, I was keeping to myself, frustrated all the time, filming the last shots of Earth's important landmarks. I had no idea I would provoke an argument with one.

"Do you really think we're bitter?" I asked, soft-toned.

"Sorry," he said. "I shouldn't have said that. I suppose your people have a right to be bitter. I know what it's like to lose your home."

I beamed an interested face.

"One night, during the war," he continued, "my families had to flee into the Derian Mountains. Hiding in a cave as Fili-Vanan warships attacked my hometown. We didn't see anything, just listened as they liquefied the buildings, killing our defenseless friends and neighbors. The next morning, there was nothing left at all. Just a giant brown lake in the ground, as if our homes had never been built."

"I'm sorry," I told him. "I wouldn't know what that's like."

I finished my coffee then, glancing down to my reflection at the bottom of the cup.

"You never got a chance to go there, did you?" he asked.

"What?"

"Earth," he said. "The A Bugs came before you were born, didn't they?"

"Actually, I was part of the last generation to be born on Earth. That's why I requested this job. I was born in a place called New York."

"Really? I've been there."

"How?"

"During the first few decades after our peoples made contact, everyone who could afford it took a trip to the *other* world. That was nearly twelve decades ago."

"Twelve decades?" I said. "You probably still have a better memory of it than I do."

"Don't you remember?"

"I was too young. We moved to Ursa just after I turned three."

"That's a shame." He nodded. "New York was an interesting city."

Smiling, "I didn't catch your name."

"It's Plong Guwat," he said, returning the smile.

"Hello, Plong Guwat," extending my hand to shake. "My name is Charles Murphy." Plong squished his hand into mine and shook, sweat dripping from green pours between my fingers. It made my palm smell for hours, but I ignored that.

"I should be getting back to work," he said, standing.

"Yeah, me too. I'm going to be shooting the Grand Canyon live."

As he washed his curd mug, I asked him, "How about meeting me here tomorrow?" And he glanced back at me, surprised. "I'd like to hear about your trip to New York."

He waved. "Sure thing."

Just before detonation, I typed Earth's coordinates into the camera and hit enter. *Filming.* Then I gazed into the blue planet—home to billions upon billions of radioactive germs—intoxicated with its puissance, its vastness. It is strange how blue Earth was compared to Ursa, not to mention large. Ursa is a small green planet with only a single continent rather than seven. It is not even half as vigorous.

Back when humans lived on Earth, there was as much tribulation between each other as there is now between alien races. Looking back, I wonder if Plong was right. I wonder if humans really are a bitter race that is not satisfied without having someone to look down to, someone to hate.

When it happened, I wasn't even watching, roaming my mind elsewhere as it exploded into the silence.

RIVERBOAT

Giant catfish like horses pull the water carriage up No Leg's River, huffing and squishing through the sickly wet, root-tied to strongropes and my steering wheel, toward the old rum house for a quick water-bread sandwich and nog.

The hornet-wood carriage was built by my father's priest, back when the river was invented. And it's been mine for the last two years, drinking me up and down the river, to the pacemaker factory on workdays and to the rum house on weekends with my friends: Chico and the Miracle Man.

Today is a weekday, but we need our drinks. "A little holiday," Chico says, and the Miracle Man has only one eyebrow but two beards. So we need a break from our sobriety, our work, our wives—especially our wives.

I take my wedding hat off and hide it under the seat of the carriage, making my sweaty head feel awkward and incomplete. It is such a nice and perfect hat, very attractive for its simple and undecorated design, but I just cannot wear it when I want to relax at the rum house. It squeezes around my head all day long until I go dizzy and can't stand up straight anymore. My mind needs to concentrate on work.

The black river has a strong meaty smell that boils up underneath the splashes and all of your clothes always contain the same meat-river smell, but we've grown used to it, and we mix the river water with vodka to make a strange, yet satisfying, drink when we can't afford the bar.

The river gets its thick taste from our cemetery underneath the river floor, where all the dead town people reside, buried under the river rocks with large water-proof head stones, and that's where my father is.

"There is spirituality in combining the river and the dead," Chico says, but the Miracle Man is missing half a thumb and never eats meat on Thursdays.

Once we get to the rum house, we tie up the horse-sized catfish and go inside, our table facing the window to watch the horse-fish bob up and around in the blue wobbling, eating our food and drinking reality into the dark corners of our minds where it can stay hidden until morning.

After the sun sinks down to a blood-eyed twilight, we travel downstream to a small island on the calm side of the river where an apartment building lives, eating cashews and staplers. Inside, we sleep with cheap women until our energy retires from us, the scent from their armpit hairs driving me back to the carriage coughing.

I leave my work-friends at the island:

"Until tomorrow," Chico says to me, but the Miracle Man hates waking up early in the morning and hates eggs even more.

And go home to dock.

My wife is sitting on the rooftop again.

Looking down at me and my riverboat again.

I don't go inside to her just yet, turn my head to the river and stare deep into the moon liquid.

And she ignores me too, gazing into the great river street, letting the only words be told by the fish, by bubbles in the water.

I close my eyes, granting the river to rock me in which ever way it feels comfortable, and the rum warms the inside of my gut, rocking me in haze-spins as I consume the thick river air.

I can hear her wishing the cancer would spread more quickly through her flesh, go from her breast deep into her insides, to her heart, squeeze the beats right out of it. At least she doesn't cry anymore, cried it all out of her. She spends her time waiting, watching my riverboat leave in the mornings and waiting for it to come back in the evenings, waiting for me to let her go, let us separate in peace.

When I open my eyes, she is gone to bed, letting the sleep heal her of her thoughts. I give the woman a few more minutes, just in case she is lying awake in bed for me, and the riverboat rocks me so gently, comfortably.

ABOUT THE AUTHOR

Carlton Mellick III is one of the leading authors in the new *Bizarro* genre uprising. Since 2001, his surreal counterculture novels have drawn an international cult following despite the fact that they have been shunned by most libraries and corporate bookstores. He lives in Portland, OR, the bizarro fiction mecca.

Visit him online at **www.carltonmellick.com**

Bizarro books

CATALOG   SPRING 2010

Bizarro Books publishes under the following imprints:

www.rawdogscreamingpress.com

www.eraserheadpress.com

www.afterbirthbooks.com

www.swallowdownpress.com

For all your Bizarro needs visit:

WWW.BIZARROCENTRAL.COM

Introduce yourselves to the bizarro genre and all of its authors with the Bizarro Starter Kit series. Each volume features short novels and short stories by ten of the leading bizarro authors, designed to give you a perfect sampling of the genre for only $5 plus shipping.

BB-0X1
"The Bizarro Starter Kit"
(Orange)

Featuring D. Harlan Wilson, Carlton Mellick III, Jeremy Robert Johnson, Kevin L Donihe, Gina Ranalli, Andre Duza, Vincent W. Sakowski, Steve Beard, John Edward Lawson, and Bruce Taylor.

236 pages $5

BB-0X2
"The Bizarro Starter Kit"
(Blue)

Featuring Ray Fracalossy, Jeremy C. Shipp, Jordan Krall, Mykle Hansen, Andersen Prunty, Eckhard Gerdes, Bradley Sands, Steve Aylett, Christian TeBordo, and Tony Rauch.

244 pages $5

BB-001 **"The Kafka Effekt" D. Harlan Wilson** - A collection of forty-four irreal short stories loosely written in the vein of Franz Kafka, with more than a pinch of William S. Burroughs sprinkled on top. **211 pages $14**

BB-002 **"Satan Burger" Carlton Mellick III** - The cult novel that put Carlton Mellick III on the map ... Six punks get jobs at a fast food restaurant owned by the devil in a city violently overpopulated by surreal alien cultures. **236 pages $14**

BB-003 **"Some Things Are Better Left Unplugged" Vincent Sakwoski** - Join The Man and his Nemesis, the obese tabby, for a nightmare roller coaster ride into this postmodern fantasy. **152 pages $10**

BB-004 **"Shall We Gather At the Garden?" Kevin L Donihe** - Donihe's Debut novel. Midgets take over the world, The Church of Lionel Richie vs. The Church of the Byrds, plant porn and more! **244 pages $14**

BB-005 **"Razor Wire Pubic Hair" Carlton Mellick III** - A genderless humandildo is purchased by a razor dominatrix and brought into her nightmarish world of bizarre sex and mutilation. **176 pages $11**

BB-006 **"Stranger on the Loose" D. Harlan Wilson** - The fiction of Wilson's 2nd collection is planted in the soil of normalcy, but what grows out of that soil is a dark, witty, otherworldly jungle... **228 pages $14**

BB-007 **"The Baby Jesus Butt Plug" Carlton Mellick III** - Using clones of the Baby Jesus for anal sex will be the hip sex fetish of the future. **92 pages $10**

BB-008 **"Fishyfleshed" Carlton Mellick III** - The world of the past is an illogical flatland lacking in dimension and color, a sick-scape of crispy squid people wandering the desert for no apparent reason. **260 pages $14**

BB-009 **"Dead Bitch Army" Andre Duza** - Step into a world filled with racist teenagers, cannibals, 100 warped Uncle Sams, automobiles with razor-sharp teeth, living graffiti, and a pissed-off zombie bitch out for revenge. **344 pages $16**

BB-010 **"The Menstruating Mall" Carlton Mellick III** - "The Breakfast Club meets Chopping Mall as directed by David Lynch." - Brian Keene **212 pages $12**

BB-011 **"Angel Dust Apocalypse" Jeremy Robert Johnson** - Meth-heads, man-made monsters, and murderous Neo-Nazis. "Seriously amazing short stories..." - Chuck Palahniuk, author of Fight Club **184 pages $11**

BB-012 **"Ocean of Lard" Kevin L Donihe / Carlton Mellick III** - A parody of those old Choose Your Own Adventure kid's books about some very odd pirates sailing on a sea made of animal fat. **176 pages $12**

BB-013 **"Last Burn in Hell" John Edward Lawson** - From his lurid angst-affair with a lesbian music diva to his ascendance as unlikely pop icon the one constant for Kenrick Brimley, official state prison gigolo, is he's got no clue what he's doing. **172 pages $14**

BB-014 **"Tangerinephant" Kevin Dole 2** - TV-obsessed aliens have abducted Michael Tangerinephant in this bizarro combination of science fiction, satire, and surrealism. **164 pages $11**

BB-015 **"Foop!" Chris Genoa** - Strange happenings are going on at Dactyl, Inc, the world's first and only time travel tourism company.

"A surreal pie in the face!" - Christopher Moore **300 pages $14**

BB-016 **"Spider Pie" Alyssa Sturgill** - A one-way trip down a rabbit hole inhabited by sexual deviants and friendly monsters, fairytale beginnings and hideous endings. **104 pages $11**

BB-017 "The Unauthorized Woman" Efrem Emerson - Enter the world of the inner freak, a landscape populated by the pre-dead and morticioners, by cockroaches and 300-lb robots. **104 pages $11**

BB-018 "Fugue XXIX" Forrest Aguirre - Tales from the fringe of speculative literary fiction where innovative minds dream up the future's uncharted territories while mining forgotten treasures of the past. **220 pages $16**

BB-019 "Pocket Full of Loose Razorblades" John Edward Lawson - A collection of dark bizarro stories. From a giant rectum to a foot-fungus factory to a girl with a biforked tongue. **190 pages $13**

BB-020 "Punk Land" Carlton Mellick III - In the punk version of Heaven, the anarchist utopia is threatened by corporate fascism and only Goblin, Mortician's sperm, and a blue-mohawked female assassin named Shark Girl can stop them. **284 pages $15**

BB-021"Pseudo-City" D. Harlan Wilson - Pseudo-City exposes what waits in the bathroom stall, under the manhole cover and in the corporate boardroom, all in a way that can only be described as mind-bogglingly irreal. **220 pages $16**

BB-022 "Kafka's Uncle and Other Strange Tales" Bruce Taylor - Anslenot and his giant tarantula (tormentor? fri-end?) wander a desecrated world in this novel and collection of stories from Mr. Magic Realism Himself. **348 pages $17**

BB-023 "Sex and Death In Television Town" Carlton Mellick III - In the old west, a gang of hermaphrodite gunslingers take refuge from a demon plague in Telos: a town where its citizens have televisions instead of heads. **184 pages $12**

BB-024 "It Came From Below The Belt" Bradley Sands - What can Grover Goldstein do when his severed, sentient penis forces him to return to high school and help it win the presidential election? **204 pages $13**

BB-025 "Sick: An Anthology of Illness" John Lawson, editor - These Sick stories are horrendous and hilarious dissections of creative minds on the scalpel's edge. **296 pages $16**

BB-026 "Tempting Disaster" John Lawson, editor - A shocking and alluring anthology from the fringe that examines our culture's obsession with taboos. **260 pages $16**

BB-027 "Siren Promised" Jeremy Robert Johnson - Nominated for the Bram Stoker Award. A potent mix of bad drugs, bad dreams, brutal bad guys, and surreal/incredible art by Alan M. Clark. **190 pages $13**

BB-028 "Chemical Gardens" Gina Ranalli - Ro and punk band Green is the Enemy find Kreepkins, a surfer-dude warlock, a vengeful demon, and a Metal Priestess in their way as they try to escape an underground nightmare. **188 pages $13**

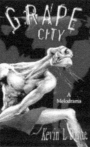

BB-029 "Jesus Freaks" Andre Duza - For God so loved the world that he gave his only two begotten sons… and a few million zombies. **400 pages $16**

BB-030 "Grape City" Kevin L. Donihe - More Donihe-style comedic bizarro about a demon named Charles who is forced to work a minimum wage job on Earth after Hell goes out of business. **108 pages $10**

BB-031"Sea of the Patchwork Cats" Carlton Mellick III - A quiet dreamlike tale set in the ashes of the human race. For Mellick enthusiasts who also adore The Twilight Zone. **112 pages $10**

BB-032 "Extinction Journals" Jeremy Robert Johnson - An uncanny voyage across a newly nuclear America where one man must confront the problems associated with loneliness, insane dieties, radiation, love, and an ever-evolving cockroach suit with a mind of its own. **104 pages $10**

BB-033 **"Meat Puppet Cabaret" Steve Beard** - At last! The secret connection between Jack the Ripper and Princess Diana's death revealed! **240 pages $16 / $30**

BB-034 **"The Greatest Fucking Moment in Sports" Kevin L. Donihe** - In the tradition of the surreal anti-sitcom Get A Life comes a tale of triumph and agape love from the master of comedic bizarro. **108 pages $10**

BB-035 **"The Troublesome Amputee" John Edward Lawson** - Disturbing verse from a man who truly believes nothing is sacred and intends to prove it. **104 pages $9**

BB-036 **"Deity" Vic Mudd** - God (who doesn't like to be called "God") comes down to a typical, suburban, Ohio family for a little vacation—but it doesn't turn out to be as relaxing as He had hoped it would be... **168 pages $12**

  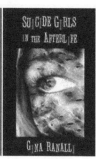 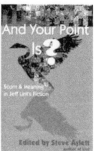

BB-037 **"The Haunted Vagina" Carlton Mellick III** - It's difficult to love a woman whose vagina is a gateway to the world of the dead. **132 pages $10**

BB-038 **"Tales from the Vinegar Wasteland" Ray Fracalossy** - Witness: a man is slowly losing his face, a neighbor who periodically screams out for no apparent reason, and a house with a room that doesn't actually exist. **240 pages $14**

BB-039 **"Suicide Girls in the Afterlife" Gina Ranalli** - After Pogue commits suicide, she unexpectedly finds herself an unwilling "guest" at a hotel in the Afterlife, where she meets a group of bizarre characters, including a goth Satan, a hippie Jesus, and an alien-human hybrid. **100 pages $9**

BB-040 **"And Your Point Is?" Steve Aylett** - In this follow-up to LINT multiple authors provide critical commentary and essays about Jeff Lint's mind-bending literature. **104 pages $11**

BB-041 **"Not Quite One of the Boys" Vincent Sakowski** - While drug-dealer Maxi drinks with Dante in purgatory, God and Satan play a little tri-level chess and do a little bargaining over his business partner, Vinnie, who is still left on earth. **220 pages $14**

BB-042 **"Teeth and Tongue Landscape" Carlton Mellick III** - On a planet made out of meat, a socially-obsessive monophobic man tries to find his place amongst the strange creatures and communities that he comes across. **110 pages $10**

BB-043 **"War Slut" Carlton Mellick III** - Part "1984," part "Waiting for Godot," and part action horror video game adaptation of John Carpenter's "The Thing." **116 pages $10**

BB-044 **"All Encompassing Trip" Nicole Del Sesto** - In a world where coffee is no longer available, the only television shows are reality TV re-runs, and the animals are talking back, Nikki, Amber and a singing Coyote in a do-rag are out to restore the light **308 pages $15**

BB-045 **"Dr. Identity" D. Harlan Wilson** - Follow the Dystopian Duo on a killing spree of epic proportions through the irreal postcapitalist city of Bliptown where time ticks sideways, artificial Bug-Eyed Monsters punish citizens for consumer-capitalist lethargy, and ultraviolence is as essential as a daily multivitamin. **208 pages $15**

BB-046 **"The Million-Year Centipede" Eckhard Gerdes** - Wakelin, frontman for 'The Hinge,' wrote a poem so prophetic that to ignore it dooms a person to drown in blood. **130 pages $12**

BB-047 **"Sausagey Santa" Carlton Mellick III** - A bizarro Christmas tale featuring Santa as a piratey mutant with a body made of sausages. 124 pages $10

BB-048 **"Misadventures in a Thumbnail Universe" Vincent Sakowski** - Dive deep into the surreal and satirical realms of neo-classical Blender Fiction, filled with television shoes and flesh-filled skies. **120 pages $10**

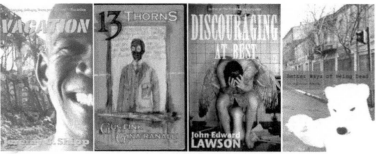

BB-049 **"Vacation" Jeremy C. Shipp** - Blueblood Bernard Johnson leaved his boring life behind to go on The Vacation, a year-long corporate sponsored odyssey. But instead of seeing the world, Bernard is captured by terrorists, becomes a key figure in secret drug wars, and, worse, doesn't once miss his secure American Dream. **160 pages $14**

BB-051 **"13 Thorns" Gina Ranalli** - Thirteen tales of twisted, bizarro horror. **240 pages $13**

BB-050 **"Discouraging at Best" John Edward Lawson** - A collection where the absurdity of the mundane expands exponentially creating a tidal wave that sweeps reason away. For those who enjoy satire, bizarro, or a good old-fashioned slap to the senses. **208 pages $15**

BB-052 **"Better Ways of Being Dead" Christian TeBordo** - In this class, the students have to keep one palm down on the table at all times, and listen to lectures about a panda who speaks Chinese. **216 pages $14**

BB-053 **"Ballad of a Slow Poisoner" Andrew Goldfarb** Millford Mutterwurst sat down on a Tuesday to take his afternoon tea, and made the unpleasant discovery that his elbows were becoming flatter. **128 pages $10**

BB-054 **"Wall of Kiss" Gina Ranalli** - A woman... A wall... Sometimes love blooms in the strangest of places. **108 pages $9**

BB-055 **"HELP! A Bear is Eating Me" Mykle Hansen** - The bizarro, heartwarming, magical tale of poor planning, hubris and severe blood loss... **150 pages $11**

BB-056 **"Piecemeal June" Jordan Krall** - A man falls in love with a living sex doll, but with love comes danger when her creator comes after her with crab-squid assassins. **90 pages $9**

BB-057 **"Laredo" Tony Rauch** - Dreamlike, surreal stories by Tony Rauch. **180 pages $12**

BB-058 **"The Overwhelming Urge" Andersen Prunty** - A collection of bizarro tales by Andersen Prunty. **150 pages $11**

BB-059 **"Adolf in Wonderland" Carlton Mellick III** - A dreamlike adventure that takes a young descendant of Adolf Hitler's design and sends him down the rabbit hole into a world of imperfection and disorder. **180 pages $11**

BB-060 **"Super Cell Anemia" Duncan B. Barlow** - "Unrelentingly bizarre and mysterious, unsettling in all the right ways..." - Brian Evenson. **180 pages $12**

BB-061 **"Ultra Fuckers" Carlton Mellick III** - Absurdist suburban horror about a couple who enter an upper middle class gated community but can't find their way out. **108 pages $9**

BB-062 **"House of Houses" Kevin L. Donihe** - An odd man wants to marry his house. Unfortunately, all of the houses in the world collapse at the same time in the Great House Holocaust. Now he must travel to House Heaven to find his departed fiancee. **172 pages $11**

BB-063 **"Necro Sex Machine" Andre Duza** - The Dead Bitch returns in this follow-up to the bizarro zombie epic Dead Bitch Army. **400 pages $16**

BB-064 **"Squid Pulp Blues" Jordan Krall** - In these three bizarro-noir novellas, the reader is thrown into a world of murderers, drugs made from squid parts, deformed gun-toting veterans, and a mischievous apocalyptic donkey. **204 pages $12**

BB-065 **"Jack and Mr. Grin" Andersen Prunty** - "When Mr. Grin calls you can hear a smile in his voice. Not a warm and friendly smile, but the kind that seizes your spine in fear. You don't need to pay your phone bill to hear it. That smile is in every line of Prunty's prose." - Tom Bradley. **208 pages $12**

BB-066 **"Cybernetrix" Carlton Mellick III** - What would you do if your normal everyday world was slowly mutating into the video game world from Tron? **212 pages $12**

BB-067 **"Lemur" Tom Bradley** - Spencer Sproul is a would-be serial-killing bus boy who can't manage to murder, injure, or even scare anybody. However, there are other ways to do damage to far more people and do it legally... **120 pages $12**

BB-068 **"Cocoon of Terror" Jason Earls** - Decapitated corpses...a sculpture of terror...Zelian's masterpiece, his Cocoon of Terror, will trigger a supernatural disaster for everyone on Earth. **196 pages $14**

BB-069 **"Mother Puncher" Gina Ranalli** - The world has become tragically over-populated and now the government strongly opposes procreation. Ed is employed by the government as a mother-puncher. He doesn't relish his job, but he knows it has to be done and he knows he's the best one to do it. **120 pages $9**

BB-070 **"My Landlady the Lobotomist" Eckhard Gerdes** - The brains of past tenants line the shelves of my boarding house, soaking in a mysterious elixir. One more slip-up and the landlady might just add my frontal lobe to her collection. **116 pages $12**

BB-071 **"CPR for Dummies" Mickey Z.** - This hilarious freakshow at the world's end is the fragmented, sobering debut novel by acclaimed nonfiction author Mickey Z. **216 pages $14**

BB-072 **"Zerostrata" Andersen Prunty** - Hansel Nothing lives in a tree house, suffers from memory loss, has a very eccentric family, and falls in love with a woman who runs naked through the woods every night. **144 pages $11**

BB-073 "The Egg Man" Carlton Mellick III - It is a world where humans reproduce like insects. Children are the property of corporations, and having an enormous ten-foot brain implanted into your skull is a grotesque sexual fetish. Mellick's industrial urban dystopia is one of his darkest and grittiest to date. **184 pages $11**

BB-074 "Shark Hunting in Paradise Garden" Cameron Pierce - A group of strange humanoid religious fanatics travel back in time to the Garden of Eden to discover it is invested with hundreds of giant flying maneating sharks. **150 pages $10**

BB-075 "Apeshit" Carlton Mellick III - Friday the 13th meets Visitor Q. Six hipster teens go to a cabin in the woods inhabited by a deformed killer. An incredibly fucked-up parody of B-horror movies with a bizarro slant. **192 pages $12**

BB-076 "Rampaging Fuckers of Everything on the Crazy Shitting Planet of the Vomit At smosphere" Mykle Hansen - 3 bizarro satires. Monster Cocks, Journey to the Center of Agnes Cuddlebottom, and Crazy Shitting Planet. **228 pages $12**

BB-077 "The Kissing Bug" Daniel Scott Buck - In the tradition of Roald Dahl, Tim Burton, and Edward Gorey, comes this bizarro anti-war children's story about a bohemian conenose kissing bug who falls in love with a human woman. **116 pages $10**

BB-078 "MachoPoni" Lotus Rose - It's My Little Pony... *Bizarro* style! A long time ago Poniworld was split in two. On one side of the Jagged Line is the Pastel Kingdom, a magical land of music, parties, and positivity. On the other side of the Jagged Line is Dark Kingdom inhabited by an army of undead ponies. **148 pages $11**

BB-079 "The Faggiest Vampire" Carlton Mellick III - A Roald Dahl-esque children's story about two faggy vampires who partake in a mustache competition to find out which one is truly the faggiest. **104 pages $10**

BB-080 "Sky Tongues" Gina Ranalli - The autobiography of Sky Tongues, the biracial hermaphrodite actress with tongues for fingers. Follow her strange life story as she rises from freak to fame. **204 pages $12**

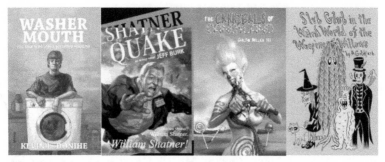

BB-081 **"Washer Mouth" Kevin L. Donihe** - A washing machine becomes human and pursues his dream of meeting his favorite soap opera star. **244 pages $11**

BB-082 **"Shatnerquake" Jeff Burk** - All of the characters ever played by William Shatner are suddenly sucked into our world. Their mission: hunt down and destroy the real William Shatner. **100 pages $10**

BB-083 **"The Cannibals of Candyland" Carlton Mellick III** - There exists a race of cannibals that are made of candy. They live in an underground world made out of candy. One man has dedicated his life to killing them all. **170 pages $11**

BB-084 **"Slub Glub in the Weird World of the Weeping Willows"** **Andrew Goldfarb** - The charming tale of a blue glob named Slub Glub who helps the weeping willows whose tears are flooding the earth. There are also hyenas, ghosts, and a voodoo priest **100 pages $10**

BB-085 **"Super Fetus" Adam Pepper** - Try to abort this fetus and he'll kick your ass! **104 pages $10**

BB-086 **"Fistful of Feet" Jordan Krall** - A bizarro tribute to spaghetti westerns, featuring Cthulhu-worshipping Indians, a woman with four feet, a crazed gunman who is obsessed with sucking on candy, Syphilis-ridden mutants, sexually transmitted tattoos, and a house devoted to the freakiest fetishes. **228 pages $12**

BB-087 **"Ass Goblins of Auschwitz" Cameron Pierce** - It's Monty Python meets Nazi exploitation in a surreal nightmare as can only be imagined by Bizarro author Cameron Pierce. **104 pages $10**

BB-088 **"Silent Weapons for Quiet Wars" Cody Goodfellow** - "This is high-end psychological surrealist horror meets bottom-feeding low-life crime in a techno-thrilling science fiction world full of Lovecraft and magic..." -John Skipp **212 pages $12**

ORDER FORM

TITLES	QTY	PRICE	TOTAL

Please make checks and moneyorders payable to ROSE O'KEEFE / BIZARRO BOOKS in U.S. funds only. Please don't send bad checks! Allow 2-6 weeks for delivery. International orders may take longer. If you'd like to pay online via PAYPAL.COM, send payments to publisher@eraserheadpress.com.

SHIPPING: US ORDERS - $2 for the first book, $1 for each additional book. For priority shipping, add an additional $4. INT'L ORDERS - $5 for the first book, $3 for each additional book. Add an additional $5 per book for global priority shipping.

Send payment to:

BIZARRO BOOKS
 C/O Rose O'Keefe
 205 NE Bryant
 Portland, OR 97211

Address

City   State   Zip

Email   Phone

Lightning Source UK Ltd.
Milton Keynes UK
UKHW041954031020
370965UK00001B/109